STEPPING THROUGH ...

C.A. ROWLAND

SHADOW DANCE PUBLISHING

INTRODUCTION

I love fantasy. From dragons to witches to fairies and all the journeys of creatures to magical worlds – reading always took me outside of reality and into new lands and adventures. Those novels and short stories were some of my favorites growing up.

I've continued reading them as an adult. As well as all kinds of other stories that transported me into the characters' worlds. However, I always seem to return to fantasy when life gives me challenges or I just want to escape. What I've also found, is that it is even more fun to write them. Creating those lands and characters allows my imagination to run free and wild.

One aspect of fantasy is that many stories have portals - or doorways or gates - that the character steps through to another dimension or land or simply to a reality that is different from where they were last standing.

For this anthology, I've put together five original fantasy stories, all of which involve portals of some kind.

The first, "The Two Trees Tavern," comes from a trip to Australia and New Zealand and my love of the land and people there. The story revolves around such a visit but the portal is really the stepping into the tavern and what happens inside the world contained within. I love the idea of a tavern where the Southern Lights shine and I know I will be writing more from the mystical tavern.

I also have a legal background and writing about a paranormal paralegal was right up my alley. In this story, I wondered how you might go about learning how to use portals if it wasn't a natural ability. As the paralegal is still learning about her talents, she was the perfect character to explore this. Add in an assignment from the creatures who run the supernatural law firm for her to represent a ghost who's on trial in a supernatural court in "Conduct Unbecoming" and the story took off.

The third story was also inspired by my trip to Australia. Being able to have an indigenous guide walk us through a bit of the song lines that tell the story of their heritage and legends was one of the most interesting experiences. "A Walk in the Song Lines" is my way of paying tribute to the willingness of the locals to share their culture with those of us who want to learn more about them.

At some point when I was writing these stories, I wondered about whether all these portals ran into each other or whether there was some system that was in place for commonly traveled places. My imagination decided that there had to be some kind of system and with it all the problems that can arise. That thought was the genesis for the "Portal Central" story.

When I think about portals, I also think about music. It has always transported me to a different state of mind or feeling - a portal in some sense. That served as the inspiration for "A Walk on the Ivories."

I hope you enjoy my fantasy portal stories included in this collection. I had great fun writing them and I hope you have just as much fun reading them.

THE TWO TREES TAVERN

Renae hiked up the dirt road, keeping her steps low to the ground to keep from raising more of the brown dust. She could see a curve to the right up ahead, bounded on both sides by what looked like giant round marbles made of yellowing grasses. The area was rocky and barren except for a few trees that were shedding their dying leaves.

She was searching for two trees - distinct ones. The folks in town had told her she couldn't miss them – one had limbs only on one side, all of which were bent over as if the tree was trying to reach down and pick up something. The other was short and squat with a few limbs that reached up and through the other one. She'd find both were so brown as to look black.

As she rounded the bend, Renae halted to wipe the sweat from her brow, sweeping her short black bangs to the side. Up ahead, she could see what she thought might be the two trees from her directions. She welcomed a cool wind that had come up with the setting of the brilliant sun that was blinding at times.

A small lake glistened in the sunlight and provided a bit of moisture to the air. The air's earthiness reminded her of the Virginia mountains, where dried leaves and branches mixed with the dwellings of the smaller creatures that made their homes within the steamy compost. She'd lived there all her adult life.

The land here was flatter, allowing her to walk each day, even though her range was getting shorter as the end of her trip neared. She was tired, but that was to be expected at her age and in her condition, the doctor had said. Still, she pushed on, fighting back against her body that had rebelled, leaving her with less and less energy.

Her light jacket was tied around her waist, not yet needed but pulled from her backpack on an earlier stop. She'd made good time and hoped to reach the Two Trees Tavern before the sun was completely gone. There was supposed to be an old church nearby as well, but she'd decided to save that for another day, if she had time on her trip and felt up to it.

For now, the old stone tavern was where she could sit and drink a cool one while watching the aurora australis, or southern, lights. Seeing them was on her bucket list, and what better place to do that than in New Zealand, where some of the darkest skies in the world would be the backdrop for the lights?

She'd long wanted to see some of the country and its neighbor, Australia, but on her terms. The outback and less crowded areas with brief stints in the cities to visit the museums and get a sense of the people.

Out alone on the trail, however, was her first love, despite the dust and lack of restaurants or comfy beds to lay her head on at night. Having the stars overhead and the scavenging sounds of animals on their nightly rounds were company enough. She quite liked making sure she had the supplies to get from one place to another, chatting up locals in the villages and towns along the way who were quite helpful.

Hiking further along, the bending outline of the trees told Renae she was in the right location. She kept moving at a steady pace, one booted foot in front of the other.

The land had turned even more barren as she moved inland with fewer trees and more scrub brush, brown and brittle. As she approached the trees, she looked to her left and saw the tavern sitting on a small hill. Steps had been chiseled out of the hill, each one almost four feet wide and two feet deep, with grayish-white rocks on each end to hold the dirt in place.

Renae counted thirteen steps to reach the entrance. Who

would go to the trouble of building the steps when walking up the incline was almost as easy? Or was that meant as a welcome to visitors?

She walked to the entrance, a wooden double door, twice her height and three times her width. It was surrounded by a mosaic of stones of yellowish-orange, brown, and tans in all shapes and sizes, as if the builder had decided to create a giant puzzle with pieces of whatever he found nearby. The black slate roof created a framework under which the stone walls rose to meet it.

She stopped for a moment, wondering if this was the entrance and if she could open the door, which looked heavy. A bronze-colored nameplate to the right side of the door read Two Trees Tavern.

Renae looked around. The townsfolk had said there were night tours for seeing the lights, but there were no other people and no sounds were coming from the tavern. Was she early? Or the only one venturing out to see the lights? None of this made sense.

She breathed in a deep breath and reached for the knob.

The door swung open easily, almost as if her touch had activated some mechanism.

Dim light poured out, and the faint notes of a bluesy country instrumental song wrapped around her.

Renae relaxed, recognizing the music as sounds she'd heard all through her travels.

She stepped inside and allowed her eyes to adjust to the darkened room. The door behind her closed with a click, taking with it the rays of sunlight from the early sunset.

It was mostly a square room with wooden walls with various doors leading to rooms between the center room Renae was in and what must have been sleeping quarters or storage areas along the building's perimeter. A fireplace assembled from more of the stones that created the building's exterior wall was in the far-right corner.

Behind the bar, glass reflected the bit of light from the metal chandeliers of lighted, glass candles. Shelving distorted the glows, with brown and clear bottles, some with long slender necks, some with short, all blocking the flickering images. It was almost as if she had stepped into a medieval tavern, but one with electricity and hopefully a few other modern conveniences like running water.

A bored-looking blond woman sat on a stool behind the bar.

Renae wove her way through the mixture of empty round wooden tables and chairs to the bar. She pulled off her backpack and leaned it up against the bar. She took a seat on a padded bar stool with woven blue and green plaid that had torn in several areas. The air was a bit musty and edged with smoke and a perfumed fragrance she didn't recognize but without any of the scent of spilled liquor on the floor or sweat from people having been in the room.

With a distracted look, the barkeep stood up and asked, "Want some grog?"

Renae had to think twice as to what grog was. All she could remember was that it related to sailing ships and pirates from a much earlier time. Rum and water, maybe?

"No, I'd like a beer. You have Speight's?"

The woman wiped down the bar with a rag as she shook her head.

"Nope. Grog or nothing."

Renae stared at her. Speight's was the beer of New Zealand. Why wouldn't this bar have it? And why only grog?

"I don't understand. Do you have coffee or maybe Lemon and Paeroa?"

With the tavern being so far off the beaten track, maybe they didn't have a liquor license for anything else.

"Sorry, the only drink is grog here."

"That's kinda weird. Why nothing else?"

For the first time, the woman looked up to stare at Renae with dead brown eyes.

"Just the way it is. You don't like it; you can sit a while or leave."

Renae was a bit taken aback at the unfriendliness, which was so unlike everyone else she'd met on the trail and in the small villages. She figured she'd stay and see the lights, then hit the road.

"This is the right place to see the aurora australis, right?"

The woman sighed.

"The southern lights. Not even the northern ones. Not even someplace lots of folks want to come to. Wish I'd never seen this place."

"Do you own it? Why don't you leave?"

The woman's face shone for a moment.

"In a manner of speaking. Why? You interested in taking it over?"

Renae leaned back against the stool's fabric cushion.

"No, I just wondered since you don't seem very happy."

The woman turned back to reach for two glasses on a shelf. She mixed up a drink and sat back down on her stool. She tilted the drink and swallowed half of it in a couple of gulps.

"I've been here sixty years today. My only wish is to be shed of this place."

Renae tried to keep the shock off her face. She would have guessed the woman was no older than forty.

"Why don't you close up and leave for a while? See the world and come back when you're ready to retire."

The woman laughed.

"Retire? It doesn't work that way here. I'm stuck until another takes over."

"Why don't you tell me about it? I am a good listener."

The woman pointed to her glass, and Renae nodded. She'd take a sip to be polite. She might even be able to collect the woman's story to add to the ones she'd already heard if she bought the drink.

After mixing the drink and adding some additional rum to her own, the woman set the glass in front of Renae.

"A toast – to new friends."

Renae lifted the glass and took a sip of the lemony rum drink, and almost coughed. It was much more potent than she had expected.

The sound of doors opening caught her attention, and she turned to the right.

Along the wall.

Three, to be exact.

A wrinkled-faced woman, her hair wrapped up in a turban, sat in a narrow closet-size room. Colorful pictures crowded every inch of the walls. The square table in front of her was covered with a flowery cloth. On top sat a crystal ball.

The second was a room with silvery walls as if they were papered with aluminum. A blond-haired girl sat smiling at her, her reflection bouncing off the walls so that her smile seemed to be coming at Renae from all directions.

The third was a wooden room, with a wizened older man seated at a small square wooden table. A pair of red and white dice laid in waiting.

Renae turned back to the woman with a question on her face.

"What's going on?"

The woman laid a gold doubloon on the counter in front of Renae.

"Comes with the drink. On the house. Pick one, any one. You'll need this."

"I don't understand."

"It goes with the pirate and grog theme," the woman said with a shrug.

Renae laughed. The woman jerked her head sharply at the sound.

"Sorry. It was just so dramatic and unreal. It caught me by surprise."

The woman relaxed a bit.

"I had the same reaction. Go check them out. You can pick one or none. Each room is different as you can see, and each has something different to give you."

Renae sipped her grog. The second taste was no better than the first sip, and she pushed it away. The rooms were intriguing. She got up and walked over to the one where the older woman sat waiting.

"Hello Renae," the woman said. "Come in and have a seat."

Renae started, wondering how she knew her name. She looked down and saw that a wooden chair had materialized in front of her. She looked around, searching for anything else that had been hidden from her.

"There is no need to worry. You can leave this room at any time. The chair was for your comfort. You can stand if you wish."

Renae moved to the chair and sat.

"What is all this? Are you a psychic or fortune-teller?"

A deep throaty laugh rang out.

"I suppose you could call me that. Or much more. I am here to make you an offer for your gold coin."

Renae remained silent, trying to take it all in.

"I can give you your past to relive again. Or rather, you can go back to any moment in your past and change it. Then continue living your old life with that change in it. I warn you that changing your past can have unintended consequences, so beware of what you decide."

As she began to think of the many times she might have

made other choices, Renae saw images filling the crystal ball. She leaned forward to get a better look.

What Renae was seeing were in fact memories.

"Yes, my dear. All of those times and more are available to you. Just say the word and pass me the coin. I'll send you off on a glorious adventure."

Renae looked up from the crystal ball.

"Will it change my health issues?"

The woman frowned.

"I am not able to see what effect any change might do, but in this as in all endeavors, some things cannot be changed."

Renae considered the woman's words. There was no underlying deceit that she could detect. She rose.

"Thank you. I have much to think about and two more rooms to visit."

The woman nodded.

"I'll be here if you chose to relive your life in a different way."

Renae rose and left the room. She turned left and walked a few feet to the second door.

As she entered, the little girl clapped her hands.

"Come in. Come in. I've been waiting so long. I have so much to tell you."

Renae smiled in spite of herself. The girl's excitement was infectious.

"And who are you?"

"My name does not matter. What I can do is offer you a way to live in your future. Would you like that? Doesn't that sound good?"

Renae had to agree it did. All the things she wouldn't be able to do like see her grandchild grow up, know that her daughter was well and happy, and see what changes happened in the world.

"It does. Is the cost here the gold coin as well?"

"Oh yes. I love gold. Can I have yours? Do you want to go with me on this journey?"

Renae wanted to say yes, if only to spend time with this young girl. Her heart felt lighter just being in her presence. She was tempted.

"If I go to the future, what would that mean for my daughter? Would I be able to see her? Will I be able to find a cure for my disease?"

The girl frowned.

"I don't know the answers. Those are in the future, and I cannot see that far. You would have to find out for yourself."

Renae considered her words.

"I will think about it."

"I hope you do. I'll be waiting for you."

Renae turned and walked out of the room. She turned left yet again, and a few steps later found herself in front of the small wooden room, unadorned with any pictures or mirrors. The wizened man sat in front of the round table with the dice.

"Come in, my dear. I've been waiting for you. Have a seat."

Once again, a chair had materialized in front of Renae. She moved to it and sat.

"I supposed you're the ghost of the present," she said.

The man giggled, and Renae laughed with him.

"Ahh, you know Dickens. It does my heart good. How is the old fellow these days?"

She stared at him, realizing that time meant something entirely different to him if he didn't know that centuries had passed.

"Charles Dickens died long ago. Are you saying he came here to visit New Zealand?"

The man waved his hand as if what she said didn't matter.

Renae sat up a bit straighter.

"I thought his trip was canceled. He was supposed to come but then didn't. The Christmas Carol was published in 1843. I don't know why you are trying to deceive me, but the two can't be related."

The man raised a finger and pointed toward the other two rooms.

"And if he had been here and chose to relive his life from a moment in his past?"

Renae sucked in a breath.

"No, that can't be."

She shook her head, unable to make sense of what the older man was implying. And yet, he had given her a clear example of how the first room might work. Was it real? Did it matter? It was mind-boggling at best.

"That would mean the woman's words were true."

The older man tilted his head to one side.

Renae took a moment to quiet her thoughts. That would mean all three of these offers might be real. But she still had not heard what the older man had to offer.

"Why are you here? What does this room mean? Assuming I am right and it is the present part of this trio of propositions."

"You are correct. This is the present. And will be the present for as long as you stay here."

Renae struggled to understand what he was saying.

"And how long would that be?"

"Only the tavern knows. You are here because it may be time for our current caretaker to move forward in her life. And leave."

Renae considered the words. She leaned forward.

"I would be stuck here, inside, for as long as I remain here?"

"That is mostly true. There will be visitors, of course. Tourists in the high season with lots more of the stories you have been collecting. You are free to go outside to see the southern lights as often as you please. You will be able to remake the tavern over in some ways, but there are restrictions.

You've seen some of that in the tavern's only drink being grog. That was an early mistake of the barkeep."

Renae sat back and watched the man.

"But I can't leave to go to town or exploring anywhere else? How will I survive without supplies"?

"This was your last adventure anyway, wasn't it? You can hike within a certain distance of the tavern, returning each day. You can even camp outside if you wish, as long as you return each day. You will be supplied with whatever you need to live."

Renae was dying anyway. Would she go stir crazy if she stayed here?

"And my health issues? Will I die here?"

The man's face softened.

"It will always be the present day for you here. The world will pass you by in time, although you can access information from your laptop of what is going on and follow your family's activities on social media. They could even come here, but they will not recognize you. And your illness will not worsen unless you leave the tavern permanently."

Renae felt stuck to her chair. The choices were overwhelming in their implications. Then there was the last choice which was to do nothing and simply live out her life and say goodbye to her daughter when the time came.

"And the dice? What are they for? Do I roll them to see if I stay or not?"

The man shook his head.

"If you decide to stay, you roll them to determine the name of the tavern and what rights you have to make changes. The lower the roll, the less you can change. The higher, the more."

Renae wasn't sure that made sense.

"And what did the bartender roll?"

"Double threes. We call that Two Trees. If you roll something other than a double, then you aren't meant to be here."

The man closed his eyes and crossed his arms on his chest.

Renae took that as a sign he wouldn't tell her anything more.

"Thank you. I have a lot to consider."

The man grunted. Renae walked absentmindedly back to the counter where the bartender sat. She wanted a real drink to wash away the acidic taste in her mouth.

She reached inside her backpack and pulled out her water bottle, taking a sip so that her tongue no longer felt glued to the bottom of her mouth. Renae turned to the bartender.

"Would you do this again?"

The woman's smile turned sad.

"I had no family to speak of when I came here. I was young and naïve. I thought having the power to remake this place and get anything I wanted was worth it. And it was for a while. I'd be glad to have you take my place so that I can live out my life somewhere else."

Renae considered her words. Her daughter had a family and was happy. They had all spent time together, knowing that Renae had a few months to live, and she wanted to live them on her terms. She would have loved to spent them with her daughter and new baby, loved to have seen the child grow up, but that wasn't going to happen. Could she instead give the woman behind the bar her life back? Was that the right turn in this trail of life?

The lure of hearing more travelers' tales was strong. And she could write those down for others to enjoy and discover. Or she could go to the future where she might be cured, or they might use her illness to save others.

What did she want? To live more? To serve?

That was truly why she had come on this journey – to a place where she could find the solitude of understanding the meaning of her life. Now she was offered a choice that would answer that question.

Renae looked down at the coin in her hand.

She'd lived a good life. If she relived a part of it, then she could lose the joy of motherhood, even as she would lose the struggles from it. She ruled that option out.

If she couldn't spend time with her family, some unknown future made no sense. She ruled that out as well.

The present – well, if Dickens went on to write his stories, so could she. With her laptop, she'd be able to type them up and send them out to the world for others to enjoy.

Or she could get back on the trail and see where it took her, free from any obligation to anyone.

Renae stood and put on her backpack.

"Good-bye. Thanks for the drink. I won't forget you."

Renae watched tears began to fall. She wasn't sure if the woman was crying because she thought Renae was leaving or relieved the decision was made, but Renae didn't stop to find out.

She moved to the rooms on the sidewall, thanking the woman and girl for their offers, and headed toward the older man. She heard the doors close as she moved away.

She entered the third room and put down her backpack.

"I'd like to roll the dice."

He opened his eyes and smiled.

"It's a good choice."

Renae set down the coin, holding onto it for a moment, then sliding it over. The man took it and reached for the dice. He placed them in Renae's hand.

She shook them. Then with a laugh, she blew on them.

"For good luck," she said as she rolled them.

Two sixes came up.

"A midnight roll," the man said. "Excellent."

Renae smiled and looked back at the bar, but it was empty. She turned to stare at the man.

"She's already on her way. The tavern is now yours. If you

want to make a change, simply roll the dice and make the wish."

Renae nodded.

"I wish I heard more of her story. Will I see you again?"

"Only when it is time for you to leave."

Renae stood up and grabbed her backpack. She walked past the first two rooms as the third door closed. She moved behind the bar, setting her gear in the corner. There was time to discover what was behind the many doors of the tavern. For now, she needed a beer and to see the southern lights.

She rolled the dice, wishing for a fully stocked bar including Speights and the other drinks of New Zealand.

Double sixes.

In a flash, the shelves' contents were replaced with bottles of vodka, gin, and other liquors, as well as soft drinks. A small refrigerator under the bar opened, inviting Renae to take a cold drink from its contents.

With a beer in hand, Renae headed to the front door.

As she opened it, her eyes feasted on a glorious display of yellows, oranges, and blues – the southern lights welcoming her.

She watched for a while until the lights began to dim and then turned to go inside.

Looking to the right, she reached out to touch the bronze faceplate which now read: The Midnight Tavern.

As she walked inside, the door clicked shut behind her. She couldn't wait to see who her first guest would be and what story they had to tell.

CONDUCT UNBECOMING

Sassafras heard footsteps racing toward her. She almost dropped her coffee cup in surprise since it was the most human approach she'd had at the paranormal law firm of Roger, Roger, and Roger in weeks.

"Sass? Wait up."

The voice belonged to the temporary receptionist, Jessie, who was hurrying down the wood-paneled hall. The liquid from Sass' mug splashed against the sides, sending the lightly caramelized and nutty smell throughout the hallway. Her office was at the back of the downtown historic building that served the law offices, so most everyone sent her floating post-it notes when they needed something. Or apparitions appeared in front of her, after giving her a brief amount of notice time.

Jessie was waving a white paper. Sassafras gave her a big smile which didn't match the feeling in her stomach that whatever Jessie had wasn't something she wanted.

'Come on in," Sassafras said as she laid her mug on a round coaster. She reached for a legal pad and pen laying on the cherry desk as she sat down in the high back swivel chair. Her office was far from the front entrance so she rarely had visitors. Small but warm from the fireplace in the kitchen, Sass found she liked the isolation from the main action in other parts of the house. Purchased one hundred years ago by the founders of the law firm specializing in matters between the human and paranormal worlds, they'd taken possession of the existing furniture, fixtures, ghosts, and all.

The house had been preserved according to the historical requirements, with a few improvements, not evident to the naked human eye, or at least to the inspectors. Some days, the halls were crowded with all manner of paranormal creatures on the prowl.

Jessie poked her head in first, with her body following.

"Mr. Am asked me to see you."

Sassafras fought to keep a frown off her face. Mr. Am handled litigation as a rule. Sass had helped out on a few cases – simple ones when no one else had been available for an arbitration and another small matter. She'd hoped she wouldn't have to do any more for a while and instead be able to focus on business transactions.

Jessie held up the paper, which flew from her hand, and hovered in the bluish haze that marked the afterlife, shifting back and forth, before it dropped to eye level in front of Sassafras.

The white paper waved at her, silently screaming for her to read:

YOU ARE HEREBY COMMANDED TO APPEAR BEFORE THE COURT OF THE REALM IMMEDIATELY TO ADDRESS THE FOLLOWING CHARGE:

Conduct Unbecoming a Ghost – Ashley McDavitch
Legal Counsel Notice Copy

WHAT THE...? Sassafras watched the page dissolve into nothingness. So quickly that she could almost believe it hadn't happened. She thought better of cursing since she never knew who or what might be listening in.

"He said you were to come to his office as soon as I delivered it to you. Will you go?"

Sassafras almost laughed but pretended to cough instead.

Jessie had been at the office for less than a week and didn't know better. No one refused a request from any of the three men whose names were on the door – not if they wanted to keep their job.

"Of course, I'll go right now."

Jessie smiled, and Sass followed her out the door and down the hall.

Heavy forest green draperies kept the street noise to a minimum while also blocking out the light for the more sensitive inhabitants. It also kept any inquisitive neighbors from seeing anything on the inside. Sass' heels tapped on the dark wood floor before being silenced by the rug that extended from one end of the room to the other.

Ambrose Rogers' office was on the second floor. Two sets of stairs – the grand staircase in the front from the reception area and the ones by Sass' office –led to the name partners' offices. A slower trek by Sass than most of those in the law firm who had abilities far exceeding hers, but she didn't mind. Mr. Am, an ancient, a fifth-generation Rogers, although Sass suspected he was older than that, had hired her as a paralegal. He seemed intent on exploring whether she had other innate capabilities that were as yet untapped.

At the top of the stairs, she turned to the right and headed to the only door. Knocking twice and then again, she pulled the door open and entered.

The paintings on the light blue walls were portraits from a different age. Sass thought at least one or two were from old masters, but she couldn't be sure. A massive mahogany desk and side chairs gave the room a weighty feeling, as if important decisions were made here daily.

The almost human-like creature behind the desk smiled at her. Mr. Am was frail-looking, thin with paper-like skin, pale but with piercing green eyes, almost cat-like that announced he was something to be reckoned with. A man, to be sure, but almost transparent except for a shock of brown hair on his head and his navy-blue suit and tie.

Mr. Am smiled.

"You took the stairs. There are numerous portals here. Why are you not taking one of them?"

Sass fought a sigh as she took the chair Mr. Am indicated she was to sit in. Finding and using portals was something her mother had tried to teach her, but she had no aptitude for them.

"I know, but I can't seem to locate one when I need it. I think you might have to give up on me ever having that skill."

Mr. Am shook his head.

"Nonsense. You have it within you to do so. I can feel it. You must not be trying."

Sassafras's back stiffened. She'd done everything she knew to learn.

"I have been watching. I know you have been working on it. But perhaps you haven't had the right persuasion."

Sass closed her eyes. She hated the thought of what was coming.

Mr. Am laughed.

"I know. But you will need this skill, so I am going to help you with it."

He paused for a moment and raised the summons again.

"This summons was the original one. The ghost is a descendant of a cousin's wife's daughter's child. A distant relative, Angela McDavitch. But still. We can't have her running around giving away firm secrets in exchange for getting out of trouble. Or worse yet, being used by someone to get to one of us. We need to defend her. I've arranged for her to meet you right before the hearing."

"I'm not a lawyer. I can't defend her, even in the paranormal courts. Can I?"

Mr. Am nodded.

"Normally no, but I have filed for a continuance since no lawyer is available to be there. The prosecuting lawyer has agreed. The hearing this afternoon is a formality only."

Sass waited. There would be a catch - something she wouldn't like.

"The only issue is that you have to go and return through a portal."

Damn.

"I've found some help for you so that you can arrive on time, but you'll need to use what you learn to get back. Tyani will be your teacher. She lives on the third floor. I wish I could go with you, but I have a client coming in a few minutes."

Sass stared at Mr. Am. He seemed almost wistful. Sass thought she'd met everyone in the office and knew the building. There was no third floor – at least not one she could see. But then, come to think of it, she'd never considered where all the apparitions who roamed the halls stayed the rest of the time.

"Tyani is a master of many arts. She has a knack for portals. She's watched you and agrees with me. You have the latent talent. You just need to learn to access it."

Someone she didn't know had been watching her. Holy crap. Who else watched her while she was at work? And she didn't want to think about it when she left. All of this was just too creepy.

"I can see from your expression that you are misunderstanding what I am saying. It wasn't anything nefarious, nor did we violate your space or privacy. Let me rephrase this. Tyani can sense certain things. I let her know you would be here. She looked in on our meeting and has confirmed to me what I already knew. We do that sometimes to make sure that we aren't asking one of our team to do more than they are capable of. It wouldn't be fair to them."

Sass wasn't sure about fairness, but she didn't like being

evaluated this way. She squirmed in her chair as she considered what to say.

"Will you at least meet with Tyani and see what she has to say? I will not force you to do something you are not ready to do, but I have great faith in you. I think your power is there for you to use once you learn a bit more."

Sassafras had to admit he was good at convincing her. It was one of the things she knew made him a lawyer who was greatly respected in the paranormal world.

"I'll see her."

"Great. She's waiting for you. If you'll go to the far wall on your left. Stand before it, knock and then walk forward. You'll be in her loft apartment on the other side."

Sass stood up and squared her shoulders. The last thing she wanted to do was disappoint Mr. Am, but she wasn't convinced she could walk through a wall. She'd have help, but still, it wasn't something she'd ever been able to do.

"Quit second-guessing yourself. You'll be fine. We're helping you get through this first portal so you know what it feels like and what to expect."

Sassafras didn't know how to say no. Mr. Am had asked her to do things she didn't think she was capable of, but then she always managed. Now, she wasn't sure she'd ever be able to do this on her own. If she tackled this assignment, she'd need a backup plan for returning to the office.

Sass took a few steps to the wall. She took a deep breath and followed Mr. Am's instructions.

As Sass disappeared from the office, she felt an over-whelming sense of nausea and disorientation. Waves of memories of being with her mother, trying to learn to use portals washed over.

She bent over at the waist, fighting to stay standing even as her equilibrium shifted from right to left. Sass wasn't sure if she was falling or staying in place.

Her feet hit solid ground, and she felt two strong arms hold her as the surges of movement left her sick to her stomach.

"Portal sickness. Child, why didn't you say so? I can help with that."

Sass felt herself being walked forward a few steps and then eased into a cocoon of blue, red, and green pillows inside a white wicker chair which seemed to swallow her. She kept her head bent over her knees as the room's swaying slowed.

"Here, I am going to touch a few pressure points to help with the sickness. Then I'll get you some tea."

Sass felt gentle hands on the inside of her arm near her wrist. As the pressure ebbed and flowed, so did the nausea. A minute later, she raised her head to stare at the woman before her.

"Tyani?"

The woman threw back her head and laughed.

"Of course. You are in my home. Where else would you be?"

Sass wasn't ready for the burst of amusement. Nor the woman before her. Ebony was the only word Sass could think of to describe the gorgeous woman before her with a mass of jet-black curls. Power and confidence oozed from her. Now she understood why Mr. Am had hated missing this meeting. Sass envied how easily she wore the brightly colored shift dress and her bare feet.

The law firm required Sass to wear attire ready to meet clients, attend meetings or be in court. The black and navy suit dresses Sass wore were confining and restrictive at best. Heels mandatory for meeting clients.

Sass' stomach settled enough so she could focus on what was around her. Every inch of the walls was covered in pictures of beaches or mountain scenes, with original art from Africa, Asia, and Europe scattered alongside those. She wished she had more time to study the works and hear the stories behind them. The few trips to the Grand Canyon and the Yellowstone

National Park had been fun, but Sass yearned to see more of the world just as this woman had done.

The furniture looked more like Sass' apartment – a mixture of pieces assembled along the way. A couch with a throw blanket of cremes and light greens invited a guest to curl up in its softness. A bookcase of bells, figurines, and an assortment of books that said come explore with me. A light incense of sage permeated the area.

Sass didn't know what to focus on first.

A faint smell of cinnamon and some herbs Sass couldn't identity announced Tyani's return with a cup of steaming liquid.

"This will help your stomach. It will also stay with you for a while since I know you need to use the portal gates today. I wish Mr. Am would have given us more time, but sometimes it is better to have less time to consider what you are about to do."

Sass wasn't sure which was worse. She sipped the tea and was surprised not by the warmth which seemed to reach out to every part of her body but by the instant relief she felt for the queasiness.

"Thank you. This is wonderful. Will you share your recipe?"

Tyani rewarded her with a huge smile.

"Yes. But I'll do one better. I have lozenges that I create from this mixture. I only have one left, but I'll give you that for your return trip. Once you are finished at court, you'll come back here, and we'll make up a batch so you always have some. Do you feel up to a short lesson?"

For the first time, Sass began to feel more confident she could handle the lesson and finding her way through the portals.

She stood up.

"Going through portals requires three things. Being able to find one when you need it, finding the one that will get you where you want to go, and being able to go through it once you know it's there. Have you ever had any sense of portal being nearby?"

Sass thought for a moment.

"I knew I couldn't use one so I never looked."

Tyani clapped her hands together.

"That's what most people don't realize. They are all around you. Now, think about what you might have seen that was on the tip of your vision or was something that seemed out of place for just a second. A flash of color. A wisp of wind where there was no open window or obvious source for it."

"I'm afraid I don't remember anything like that."

Tyani nodded and moved to the center of the room.

"You came in through a portal, and in fact, there is more than one here. Can you find one?"

Sass' heart started to pound. She stared at the door and then slowly around the room, trying to relax her shoulders as her eyes floated over the pictures and furniture. A flash of light blinked, but Sass realized it was made by her body shielding light from a vintage Tiffany lamp and then moving past it.

"I don't see anything."

Tyani moved to the couch and sat on one end.

"Try closing your eyes and reaching out from within. Banish those thoughts of what happened to you as a child and just relax into this. There is no right or wrong way. We all find the portals in our own way. And if you don't find one today, we'll make arrangements to have someone meet you at court to bring you back."

Sass could feel some relief from the pressure to find an entry point release, but she didn't want to disappoint Mr. Am.

"Open your eyes. When you think you see something, move to it and reach out. Your fingers will feel a tingling as you touch the veil between the places. I'm going to check my pantry to make sure I have all we need to make the tea drops when you return."

Tyani rose and headed to the kitchen. Sass heard drawers and a door open and shut. She moved around the room.

A flash of light that might have been another shadow on the bookcase. She reached forward – nothing.

A soft bit of air tickled her arm and she turned, reached out to a wooden spear hanging on the wall – nothing.

Sass sat back down in the wicker chair. She closed her eyes and willed her body to relax. Her mother had taught her to breathe and focus on her favorite teddy bear. How long had it been since she'd taken just a minute or two to do that?

Her head cleared, and it seemed her consciousness reached out. A flash of red by the Tiffany lamp caught her mind's eye. Was it just a reflection or something more?

Sass opened her eyes and moved to the lamp, stepping to the side where she'd seen the flash. She hesitated and then touched the space. A hint of nausea ran up her arm. A flood of relief, joy, and trepidation filled her.

She turned to head to the kitchen only to see Tyani standing there, smiling.

"Congratulations. That didn't take long."

"My mother taught me some things growing up. I had forgotten them."

Tyani nodded and turned back to the kitchen.

"Now find another one. Each portal has a particular resonance and clue. Some are easier to find than others."

Sass coughed as she laughed. She began moving around the room - the movement and the simple act of chuckling had released more stress.

Over the next half hour, Sass found three more. One with a faint impression of a doorknob when standing in front of it. Another was a framed map with an "X" marked on it where the "X" became almost a 3-D vision. The third was a doll sitting on the bookcase who extended a hand when Sass stepped up to her.

"Good job."

Tyani was back and walked across the room to the couch to sit down.

"What have you learned?"

Sass moved back to the chair.

"I think the trick is to look closely and from different angles. I almost didn't see the doorknob until I slowed down. More importantly, I had trouble finding them when I was nervous."

"You're going to do fine. The nervousness will diminish as you use the portals more. And as you see more of them, they will become easier to spot. Mr. Am contacted me. It's time for you to head to court."

Sass could feel her nerves kick back in.

Tyani walked to the closet and pulled out a navy jacket, Sass' purse, and the brown leather laptop bag.

"Mr. Am had it sent up so you wouldn't have to go back to your office. This way, I'll open the portal for you so you arrive where you're supposed to be. You've mastered finding them. We'll use the next lesson to help you find the ones you need to travel to a particular place."

"And getting back?" Sass asked as she put on her jacket.

"Do you have your iPhone in your purse?"

Sass unzipped the main compartment and pulled out the phone.

"In the apps section, download "Para GPS."

Sass did a double-take.

"What?"

"It's a real app. Search for it and download it."

Sass did as instructed. When it was downloaded, she opened it.

"Okay, now what?"

"Type in TT57."

Sass typed on the small keyboard. The address came up with a green Go button showing.

"When you are ready to return, find a portal, then just push Go. It'll bring you right back here. It's got a built-in notification so I'll know you have accessed it. It's my private portal access so don't abuse it."

Sass was barely listening but clicked the side button on her phone and the screen went dark. She memorized the numbers and letters, just in case. She was as ready as she could be.

Tyani walked to the front door and opened it. In front of Sass was an opaque swirling mist.

"I almost forgot."

Tyani handed Sass a small square lozenge, the size of a piece of gum.

"The tea you drank should help with the trip there. Chew on this a few seconds before you start back."

Sass took the wedge and secured it in her pocket. She wouldn't take off her jacket, so it was the safest place for what she knew she'd need.

"Remember to look around you. There can be helpful indicators in the most obvious places at times."

Sass stepped through the door. The lack of moisture in the haze, the oppressiveness of the unmoving fog, and the absence of any sound unnerved her. The lack of sensory details seemed to her like an amputated limb that still seems to send sensations to the brain. She kept trying to find a smell to lock onto even as her stomach began to churn.

She kept moving, a few steps forward and she stepped onto a solid white tile floor, barely visible through the lurking fog wisps that seemed to be everywhere. The churning stopped. Sass was so thrilled the tea worked that she almost walked through a ghost floating in front of her. She was rewarded with a ghastly snarl.

Sass refocused. Being late was not an option in human court, and she doubted the paranormal court was any different.

She focused on the Court's location listed on the summons and headed down the hall.

As she neared where she thought the hearing room would be, Sass saw a ghost fidgeting near a grayish stone-like wall. Beside the ghost were a few perches instead of wooden benches to accommodate the otherworldly inhabitants. Sass licked her lips - no sounds, no smells, no taste here either.

Nearer to the door, Sass saw a blue fog that seemed to shift and shape into hazy forms, much like the woman shape she assumed was Angela.

She approached and almost stuck out her hand to shake until she realized that wasn't possible.

"Are you Angela?"

"Yeah. You're late. We're up next. You gonna get me out of this jam? I thought Uncle Am was handling this case?"

Sass wasn't sure which to answer first. Uncle Am wasn't a concept she'd ever considered, although she knew he had had more than one family.

"I am here because Mr. Am couldn't be here, so he requested a continuance. This is a formality since the other side has already agreed to the delay. Mr. Am will represent you in the actual hearing on the merits of the case."

Angela frowned as Sass moved past her to the entrance.

Someone had caused the miasma to look like double doors similar to those within an ornate theater house where Sass had attended a concert once. These stood before Sass, but instead of an usher, a seven-foot-tall ghost guarded the entrance. A black silk sheet marked it as an official of the court, together with its silver badge that Sass had heard could be used to dissolve any of those who chose to enter with nefarious designs or simply tried to gain access without authorization. Or escape. It appeared to be genderless.

Sass got in the line of those waiting approval for entry as Angela floated over to hover next to her.

"Name?" the guard asked in a throaty voice that could have been male or female in its earthly incarnation.

"Angela McDavitch."

"I'm Sassafras Prorano. I'm here on Ms. McDavitch's behalf."

"And you are here for?" it asked.

Sass produced the summons and the security officer reviewed it, then looked at her for a reaction and then studied it again.

"It's half past the time you should have been here," it said. "The court will not approve."

"I'm sorry. I could not have arrived more quickly," Sass said.

"Humph."

She wasn't sure why he didn't believe her. Time seemed to be relative here and Sass was on time, at least she thought she was. Apparently, she should have taken a faster portal to arrive earlier.

"Can we go in?" Sass asked.

"I suppose. But don't blame me if you are reprimanded for being late," it said.

Sass did her best to present herself positively. She looked over at Angela. Where her shoulders would have been, she now slumped in what she hoped was a submissive pose, leaving the sheet to gather on what served as a tiled floor.

"Don't slump. I know this is just procedural, but we don't want to anger the judge," Sass whispered.

No response.

Sass walked forward. She noted that Angela rose slightly, moved around the guard, and drifted through the doors. Sass took the time to compose herself for whatever was on the other side. She wove in between the many ghosts moving through walls and doors who never seemed to considered that another might need to move past them.

Inside, Sass was relieved to see that the area by the door was clear.

Angela took the lead and glided forward to the back row of the bench perches, free-floating lines for those waiting to be called. The benches stretched ahead like an earthly courtroom, stopping halfway with a small gated fence marking the other half of the room.

Sass checked out the others who had been brought here, wondering what they'd done. There were large, broad ghosts. Smaller ones. Shorter ones. All in the white sheet uniform that identified their otherworldly classification. The stark white boundaries that marked where the court seemed to well, hold court, were some distance away. Until they moved, the ghosts seemed almost to meld into space, unseen.

Too far back to hear most of what was said in the current case, and busy thinking about what she'd do when she was finished, Sass almost missed the call.

"Case 7287665A4, Office of Case Management vs. Angela McDavitch. Are the offender and counsel here?"

"Yes, I'm here," Sass said as she moved forward to the table on the right of the room. She could feel Angela bristle at being called an offender, but there wasn't anything Sass could do about that.

Angela sashayed forward beside Sass, the edges of her sheet fluttering in the wake of her movement. If nothing else, Sass had to give her credit for the style of her approach.

As Sass walked forward, counsel for the last defendant turned from the table. The man was slightly taller than Sass, with long brown hair pulled back in a ponytail. He smiled as he stepped aside for her to reach the table, their shoulders briefly touching. Sass felt a tingle run through her arm before her attention was drawn away. The clerk moved before the elevated desk in the center of the wall before her. It was a darker opaque structure stretching across the entire area. A ghost sat to one side with what looked to be some kind of recording mechanism and was empty on the other side.

"Officer Droyd, are you ready to present your case?" the clerk of the court, decked out in a black silk sheet, asked.

Sass looked over at the graying official. She'd never been in the Case Management offices either, but she'd watched the officer in the few minutes before their case, lording it over the others who were talking to the newly dead like Angela, although she'd not heard his actual words. Sass was glad they had an agreement on the continuance. She'd rather not have to represent anyone against the prosecutor.

"Angela McDavitch, is your representative here?" the court official asked.

"I'm here, your honor. I am supporting Ms. McDavitch in this matter," Sassafras said.

"We are not familiar with you. Are you admitted to the paranormal bar for this Court?"

Sass felt the color rising in her cheeks. She hadn't expected this to be so adversarial for a simple hearing.

"No, I'm not. The lawyer for the defendant could not be here. It is my understanding that there is an agreement on a continuance so that Mr. Rogers can be here for the actual hearing at a later date."

"Officer Droyd, is there such an agreement?" the clerk of the court asked.

"Yes."

"I will consult with Judge Burmay."

"No need, I am here. The case will proceed. There will be no continuance. I'm tired of these lawyers thinking they can do this without consulting the court. We'll proceed now."

Sass almost choked as the judge floated through the wall to hover above the desk in front of her. She wasn't prepared to argue the case.

"Young lady, I know you are not a lawyer, but this is a

simple case so the court will grant a waiver for you to act on behalf of your client if Ms. McDavitch agrees," the judge said.

Angela brushed up against her.

"Can you do this? Can you call Uncle Am?"

"We can sentence you now if you'd prefer Ms. McDavitch. I wish to clear my docket today," the judge said.

Sass looked at Angela who despite being a hazy figure was looking desperate.

"I'll help you. Don't say anything unless I ask you something. Got it?"

Angela bristled at the tone, but Sass couldn't tell her that she had no idea how she'd handle this."

"No response? Or do you want to be incarcerated for the rest of your remaining afterlife?" the judge asked.

"Go ahead," Angela said, although Sass could hear in the words a fierce retort that she'd held back, hanging there, ripe and ready to fight back.

"You may be perched," the court official said.

Sass took a seat in a hard chair behind the table while Angela floated back to a wooden perch behind the table.

"Officer Droyd, please proceed," Judge Burmay said.

"Thank you, your honor. My office oversees the newly dead and assigns those to positions who wish to remain close to their loved ones. For a period, on the earthly plane. As you know, this is strictly regulated, and those who are assigned are under constant surveillance to make sure they comply with all the rules set by those in charge of this realm," Officer Droyd said.

"Yes, yes. We know all that. Move it along," Judge Burmay said.

"Understood, your honor. I say all that since the accused are generally here for their first offense, as in this case, and they do not seem to realize that we take all those rules and regulations very seriously. Without them, the earthly realm would become quite unmanageable and chaotic with spirits run amuck."

"True. Get to the facts, please."

For the first time, Sass began to have some hope that she could help Angela. The judge wasn't taking any flak from anyone. His response to Sass and Angela wasn't personal. She calmed her nerves a bit, thankful the prosecutor was giving a summary since she'd barely looked at the case and facts.

"Yes, your honor. Two earthly cycles ago - days in that realm – the accused watched over her younger sister, Jackie. This was part of her assignment as a newly deceased, and due to the fact that the accused's mother was widowed and still distraught over her daughter's untimely motorcar accident, we felt this appropriate. Even under the circumstances," Officer Droyd said.

"The circumstances?" Judge Burmay asked.

Sass jumped up.

"Objection. How my client died is not relevant to the matter at hand. She has already been through any disciplinary or corrective proceedings regarding that. Court of the Realm vs. James Dean."

Sass had studied the case one afternoon when she wasn't busy since she'd been fascinated to see there was an other-worldly case on him. Now, she wished she'd read a few more cases.

"That's hardly relevant case law," Officer Droyd said. "Besides, we are here on a similar matter."

"I'll allow you a bit of latitude here since this is your first case before me," Judge Burmay said, "But make sure it's related, without some long-winded explanation or any theatrics."

Angela coughed to cover the giggle, which brought another admonishment from Sass. "Hush. You are not helping."

"Is your client well enough to proceed?" Judge Burmay asked.

"Yes, your honor. I believe she may have reacted to a bit of dust she brought with her, having recently been on the earthly plane."

"Very well, continue Officer Droyd."

"As I was saying, Ghost McDavitch was at her prior living quarters. Her earthly mother had fallen asleep on the couch. The four-year-old child, Jackie, was on the floor playing with some blocks nearby when she let out a screech. Instead of comforting the child, the accused flew backward through the chimney, causing the child, who is still young enough to recognize her presence, to begin screaming. Very unbecoming behavior," Officer Droyd said.

"I was just surprised. What's wrong with an honest reaction?" Angela asked.

"Hush," Sass said with a glare over her shoulder to her client. "Objection, your honor. The Officer is stating its opinion rather than simply the facts. Judgment is supposed to be reserved to the Court."

"I agree. Please confine your remarks to the facts," Judge Burmay said. "Those events hardly rise to the level you are suggesting. The newly dead may have been surprised and responded accordingly."

"That's right," Angela said.

Judge Burmay shifted in Angela's direction, and Sass wished she could muzzle her. "Your counsel will have time to dispute the case. Representative, please control your client."

Officer Droyd continued after receiving a nod from the Judge. "We would not have brought the charges if that had been the only offense." Droyd paused. "After flying backward through the chimney, the accused momentarily materialized enough to rub soot all over the white sheet, making her visible to any number of earthly beings."

Angela heard a collective gasp in the courtroom. "It was an accident. How would I know that could happen?" Angela asked while Sass' frown deepened. How was she supposed to represent someone who didn't listen to her?

"That is very bad indeed," Judge Burmay said. "Was there confusion or any chaos caused by this?"

"No, luckily, the accused remained close to the home where she had lived in her earthly life," Officer Droyd said as it consulted its notes in the case file. "However, it was what came after that is the true issue at hand."

Sass heard Angela suck in what would have been a breath if she was alive. So this was what they were after.

"The accused lit a cigarette and smoked it. That was bad enough. And we are still investigating how she learned to hold such a material object for that length of time without extensive training," Officer Droyd turned towards Angela as if daring her to explain. This time she kept silent.

"Apparently, she has more to study about this type of action since she dropped the cigarette, her sooty sheet began to burn, and she was forced to douse herself in a water bucket to put out the fire."

Sass turned to look at Angela, who hung her head.

The courtroom had gone silent. All of those waiting were edging forward for closer perches. None wanting to miss any lurid detail. Lack of decorum as a ghost was highly offensive behavior.

"Even this was not her worst offense. In her sodden, dirty sheet, she returned to the house, found some liquid spirits, and drank them. As you know, alcohol and any drugs, including nicotine, are strictly forbidden to ghosts – on the earthly plane as well as here. The accused materialized in order to imbibe, became quite inebriated, then de-materialized as she bounced off walls and into furniture, turning her prior home into a mad scramble as the earthly bound struggled to understand what was happening. Except for her young sister, who thought it was a game and laughed at her antics.

Hardly the example we expected her to be," Officer Droyd said.

Sass thought it sounded much worse than it might have been. Angela didn't seem like a hardened criminal, and she might have been trying to turn the situation into something less scary for her sister. Maybe not the best choice. But something she could argue.

"Is that all?" Judge Burmay asked.

"There were reports all over the neighborhood of strange happenings that night. Whether it was a hysterical response or whether Ghost McDavitch was responsible? We haven't been able to ascertain any direct connection," Officer Droyd said.

"Those are irrelevant if there's no proof they were related to my client. Move to strike, your honor," Sass said.

"So stricken. You will keep your remarks to the facts," Judge Burmay said. "Anything else you'd like to add, Officer Droyd?"

"No, your honor.

"Representative Prorano, please present any defense," Judge Burmay said.

"Your honor, may I have a word with my client before we proceed?"

Judge Burmay stared at Sass and nodded.

"What happened?" Sass whispered.

"It was a minor slip. I thought no one would see me beside the shed out behind the house. I was humiliated at having caught myself on fire. I needed some relief. The rest, well, it just sort of happened."

"Don't say anything more, no matter what they say. Do you hear me?"

"Yes."

"Thank you, your honor. We're ready to proceed."

Judge Burmay waved for Sass to continue. It gave her a moment to compose herself.

"If it pleases this court, my client is newly dead. She was

surprised and startled by the young earth child's response. It is a common mistake, and I understand the behavior normally results in a reprimand and re-training rather than prosecution." Sass paused. "The cigarette and alcohol were coping mechanisms in her earthly life, as evidenced by the fatal accident that resulted in her untimely death. She clearly has addiction issues and should receive counseling for those rather than something harsher."

Angela started to float forward, but Sass moved so that her sheet seemed to hold her back.

"Does your client wish to address the Court?" Judge Burmay asked.

"A moment with my client again, please?" Sass asked.

The judge nodded.

Sass turned away from the front of the courtroom, pulling Angela along. "What are you doing?" she whispered. "Do you want to be put away? Don't you realize I am trying to save you?"

"Save me. I was trying to entertain my sister, not scare her. You're making me sound like some deranged, crazy presence. I'm not. I just made a, well, a couple of, mistakes," she said.

"If you start explaining and waste the court's time, it will only get worse for you. Believe me, judges have heard it all. They hate whiners and excuse-makers. The best you can do is keep quiet or accept the blame for your actions," Sass said.

Angela considered all this.

"Ms. Prorano, I have other cases today," Judge Burmay said.

"Now or never."

"I'll accept the blame," Angela said.

Sass and Angela turned back towards the judge.

"I am sorry for my actions. I am newly passed over and am still learning. I over-reacted to all that was happening, but I really wanted to be there for my sister, so she doesn't make the same mistakes I made in my earthly life," Angela said. "It won't happen again."

"Anything else from either side?" Judge Burmay asked.

All nodded.

"The court will take a short recess while I consider the case."

After a time, Judge Burmay sailed back into the courtroom and settled onto his perch overlooking the gallery. He looked at both the prosecution and defense areas.

"I've carefully considered the facts and am prepared to give my finding." He paused. "I'm impressed that the accused has taken responsibility for her actions. However, they were egregious. And young ghost, you are so busted. Sixty cycles of hard labor in the white sheet processing compound."

Poof. The Judge disappeared.

Sass hung her head as Angela gasped.

"Sixty cycles? I thought they'd give me probation."

What appeared to be an officer of the court glided to hang in front of Angela.

"I did too. I'm surprised."

"Please come with me," the officer said.

"My uncle's gonna hear about this," Angela said as she was led away.

Sass watched her leave through a side door that opened when the officer approached it. She had no idea how she'd explain all this to Mr. Am.

"Next case, please."

Sass realized she needed to leave and find the portal back. She bundled up her things, walked out of the courtroom, and turned right, trudging back down the hall she'd entered from. There had to be a portal where she'd come through. She'd start her search there.

She clasped her hands together to keep them from shaking. She'd lost her first case in the Court of the Realm.

Tears threatened and Sass looked for a bench. She needed to calm her nerves and emotions if she was going to find her way back.

She spied one up ahead and hurried toward it. Sass was back in the rotunda area of the facility. The openness gave her the feeling that she could hide against a wall for a few minutes. She sank onto the stone seat which was squishy until it firmed up beneath her, and laid her purse and laptop case down.

"So, how are you doing?"

Sass looked up and saw the man she'd seen in court.

"My client was convicted. Not a good day."

He smiled, but it was a kindly smile.

"Don't worry too much. Judge Burmay almost always convicts the newly dead. He says it serves a point and makes them more responsible."

"You mean I never had a chance?"

"You could say that. But sixty cycles, which is sixty days in our timeframe, is a short sentence. Why wasn't Ambrose here? I was hoping to have a word with him after the hearing?"

"You know the Rogers?"

Sass realized that it was a dumb question even as the words were leaving her mouth.

"Sorry, of course you do, everyone does. He had a client meeting he couldn't miss," Sass said.

"And Angela is family, right?"

Sass' heart dropped as she put the pieces together. Mr. Am had known what would happen and didn't want to deal with the family drama that would follow.

"Yes. I guess I understand a bit more now."

The man laughed.

"I'm Jeremy Jacobs. And before you ask, yes, I'm with Jacobs and Jacobs. My family firm is much like the Rogers firm."

He extended his hand. Sass took it, feeling the same bit of a tingle she'd felt as his shoulder had touched hers in court.

"It's good to meet you," Sass said.

"Are you headed back to the earthly realm?"

Sass nodded as she slipped the lozenge from her pocket and popped it into her mouth.

"I am. I need to find a portal. I haven't been here before, so I'd better start looking."

"I hope to see you again," Jeremy said. "And if its portals you need, this place is full of them. Check out the map above your head for earthly destinations and the ones to your right and left for the other types of destinations. They are posted throughout if you are ever back here again and need one."

Sass watched Jeremy walk away and hoped he was right about the two of them running into each other at a different time. She calmed her mind by focusing on her teddy bear again. She stood, turned and stared at what had been right where she needed it. Tracing a line from her position to a portal on the other side of the room, she turned and moved away.

The portal was a doorknob one, similar to its match in Tyani's loft. She pulled out her phone which was still on the Para GPS section, and pushed Go.

This time the trip seemed to go faster. As Sass stepped into Tyani's living room, she was greeted with a huge smile that warmed her heart. She felt no after-effects of the travel.

"I am guessing the hearing was longer than expected?"

Sass nodded.

"Not surprising. Let's meet next week for another session, and we'll make up the tea for you to take. Here's a list of what you'll need. Fresh herbs are best for this. I'll text you a few dates/times, and we can schedule something."

Sass thanked her before looking back. Tyani opened the portal door for her, and Sass walked through to her office. She was glad to be back on home territory where she knew what was what and where it was.

For the next hour, Sass prepared a written report to Mr. Am

regarding the meeting and submitted it to him. He replied back with *"Good Job"* scrawled across it and a note that read: *Please keep up your training with Tyani. She indicated you are an excellent student and are mastering the use of portals quickly.*

After feeling like the court hearing had been a disaster, Sass was relieved to know that Mr. Am approved of what had happened with Angela and her work with Tyani. She felt like she might have gained a friend in Tyani, at least she hoped so. Maybe, with her help, she could master the use of portals after all.

WITHIN THE SONG LINES

Meyani wandered near the outside of the round cultural center building. The roofline extended over the sidewalk, allowing her to move around the sandy-brown mud-brick building without the sun's rays beating down on her. The edge of winter was still warm, with swarms of flies not yet banished so that she saw the world through a web of black mesh.

As she walked inside, she lifted her head netting so it settled on the wide brim of her beige hat. Meyani struggled to imagine how the center represented Kaniya, the woma python woman, within its shape - her body being made of mud for the walls and the roof being her spine.

Although cooler here, the leaf-shaped ceiling fans brought a welcome relief as she progressed between the exhibit presentations. Placards with pictures and written words marking the area's history near Ulura, or Ayers Rock as some called it. The large sandstone rock formation's color ranged from beige to orange to a deeper orange during a day's cycle, in the southern part of the Northern Territory of Australia. While looking like a smooth mound from far away, Meyani had seen the deep red sandstone fissures and cave openings that marked a much more complicated structure up close.

She walked the complex twice, seeing small details such as a map that she'd overlooked and a few drawings that were so much a part of the wall she'd walked past them. Hearing a few trilling bird calls from the outside amid the quiet conversations of others like her from the tour, she knew her time here was limited.

Still wanting to find a souvenir of the place she'd felt so drawn to the last few days, she moved around the polished desk that held a checkout register and a few booklets. On the far side was a glass cabinet with beaded bracelets and necklaces. A few painted rocks were nestled among other trinkets. As she stared down, the boomerang in the middle toward the back kept drawing her attention.

The shape was curved so that it would have formed one half of a box edge if connected to a second one. Tan wood with dotted lines that Meyani knew symbolized stars or sparks with an ancestral connection to the earth, was faded with age. A stylized and exaggerated jumping kangaroo, almost indiscernible from the purple background, lunged between the circles of dots on each end.

A woman with curly grayish-black hair, her skin dark so that it would protect her from the unrelenting sun, approached her from the desk behind the counter. She could have been any of the local women she'd seen on the tour explaining the meaning of stories relating to Ulura or the cave drawings–except for her eyes.

Bright, intelligent, and interested. A calmness seemed to emanate from the woman. That and a knowingness that Meyani had no reason, other than a feeling, to recognize.

"What are you searching for?" she asked.

Meyani had the feeling the woman was asking about more than just her search for a keepsake from her trip. She paused.

"My identity. Who I really am."

The woman smiled so broadly Meyani wasn't sure how to react.

"You have doubts as to what you know so far?"

Meyani nodded.

"My mother died when I was young. I don't know about her family or my heritage, although I have been told there may be a connection to this land. I've always felt a draw here too, but I'm not sure why."

The woman was silent.

"Most have no idea where they are in life or what they want. You are lucky to know and be on that journey. Without your ancestry, the best we can do is see what you attract."

The statement made no sense, but Meyani relaxed and decided to be candid.

"I don't seem to know what to do next or where to go."

The woman studied Meyani and reached across the counter to touch her bare arm just above her wrist. Whatever the woman felt gave her some answer, and she reached down to open the glass case. She took the boomerang Meyani had been eyeing and placed it on top of the counter.

"If you truly want to journey, this will help you with the way in."

The woman said no more as Meyani stared at the piece of wood which was weathered on both ends and looked to have been used many times.

"So what? I throw it?"

"In a way. You carry it with you. When the time is right, you send it off to open the gate."

Meyani couldn't believe what she was hearing. It made no sense.

"A gate opens? And I walk through?"

The woman smiled again.

"I sense a bit of my heritage in you. The gate or a door is something you understand? Yes? You will see it and know it when it happens. Enter quickly, for you will only see where the boomerang passed through for a short time. After that, you will not find it on your own."

Meyani almost walked away. It sounds so incredible. But she'd asked and had gotten an answer.

"And when I want to come back from wherever this takes me?"

The woman shrugged.

"When it is time for you to return, the boomerang will show you the way back."

Within the words, Meyani sensed the warning. She could not expect to return unless she finished the journey that started with the item sitting before her.

She picked it up, felt the smoothness of the polished wood. It felt heavier than she had imagined and carried a sense of time as if it was older and maybe of a different time. Which made no sense either as they wouldn't like selling some that carried this value.

Meyani took a deep breath and made her decision.

"How much do I owe you for it? It looks old and valuable," Meyani said.

The woman grinned.

"Beginning such a trek should be launched with a gift rather than an exchange of commerce. The boomerang is yours for as long as you need it. When you are done with it, leave it with someone you feel will honor it, or in a sacred place. Someone else will use it, or it will find its way home. Its value cannot be paid in coin."

Meyani thanked her. She wanted to hug the woman but had no idea if that was acceptable in the aboriginal culture. Instead, she clasped the woman's hand when it was offered, hoping to convey her gratitude.

She took the boomerang and walked out before she realized she had no idea how to throw it. Or if she did, how she would catch it or at least not hurt herself in the process. Meyani turned back to ask the woman, but there was no one there.

She looked into the display area. Odd that she was gone so quickly. It had only been a minute, but the woman must have made her way out through the other side of the round room.

Meyani made her way back around the outer corridor of the building and then exited. Feeling sweat form on her forehead, she wiped it with her sleeve. Several boys were kicking a ball around in the dusty area near the parking lot.

She moved to a wooden bench and watched them, marveling at their ability to run in the heat with the flies all around. Dust swirled as they chased each other until the ball was fired close to Meyani.

Reaching down, she caught the rolling ball and held it for the young man who chased it.

"Thanks, lady."

He picked up the ball, glanced at her again, and then began to run. Only to stop and turn back.

"Hey, is that your boomerang?"

Meyani smiled.

"It is. I just received it. Do you want to look at it??

He raced over.

"Sure. Can I hold it? It looks very old."

Meyani nodded, handing it to him.

"It's a returning boomerang. Do you know how to throw it?"

"You're right, it is. And I've never tried to throw one. Have you? Maybe you could teach me."

The young man's chest puffed out.

"I have thrown these many times, although not one decorated quite like this. It is old. I can tell from the feel of the wood. Been used many times. I can show you how. Come, follow me."

Meyani stood and followed the boy across the dusty field. He dropkicked the ball to one of the other boys, yelling, "I'll be back."

The boy kept looking back to make sure Meyani was behind him. When he reached a deserted part of the dusty landscape, he turned and smiled. Meyani realized he was older with dark eyes shining with more maturity than she'd first thought. He was as tall as she was but with wider shoulders and muscular arms.

"We can practice here."

Meyani joined him.

"If you're going to teach me, I think I need to know your name? I'm Meyani."

The teenager reached out the hand not holding the boomerang.

"I'm Jarrah."

Meyani shook his hand, noting his firm grip.

"Now, what do I need to know about throwing?"

Jarrah's face turned serious. He knelt and pulled a bit of green weeds. He tossed them in the air and watched how they fell.

"A small wind is best, like today. You are right-handed, correct?"

Meyani nodded, mesmerized by the boy's seriousness in explaining each detail.

"You must throw to the right of the oncoming wind. Did you see the way the grass fell when I threw it in the air? That's how you tell which way to throw."

Jarrah turned to make sure Meyani was paying attention and then continued. He turned to his left.

"Stand by me. See the wind is flowing directly in my face? Now turn forty-five degrees to the right."

"Why this way?"

Jarrah smiled.

"We are throwing around the wind. We will throw it to the right of the wind, and if we do this correctly, it will return on the left side."

Meyani wasn't sure she understood why that would work, but she didn't question him.

"Now. You grasp the boomerang at one end and hold it so the rest is extended up. The curved side should always be facing you, and the flat side facing away from you. Can you see that?"

Jarrah showed Meyani how he was gripping the end and where the curved side was.

"Grip the end with a pinch between your thumb and index finger. We are going to throw this by flicking our wrists backward and then snapping it forward. The motion will pull the boomerang out of your hand and create the spin it needs."

Meyani wasn't at all sure she could throw this piece of wood with any effect. Jarrah next showed her the footwork. Pivoting on the right foot outwards, then lifting her left leg so all the weight was on it, then stepping forward on the left leg as she threw.

Jarrah made her go through the process without actually throwing anything. It felt awkward and impossible to remember all of the parts of the throw at first. But she'd played softball in high school, and trying out for pitcher felt somewhat the same as far as the motion.

"That's it, you're getting it," Jarrah yelled.

Meyani smiled.

"Think we can try it for real?"

Jarrah nodded.

Meyani stepped a few paces away and flung the boomerang – straight into the ground.

Jarrah erupted into laughter.

Meyani's face went hot.

"No. No. I did the same thing the first time I threw one. Here. Let me show you."

Jarrah came over. Meyani stood as he maneuvered her arm through the process.

"See, you are throwing too late. As you raise your arm and it is still above your shoulder, you must pop your wrist. The spin is more important than the strength in the beginning."

Jarrah stepped away, and Meyani tried again. This time, the boomerang went further, and Jarrah ran to retrieve it.

"Let me have the grip, but put your hand on mine. You'll feel the difference in how I throw it."

Meyani moved in front of Jarrah so that the two were close but not touching except at the end of the boomerang. They went through the motion again without throwing it.

"Now, try to let it go at the same time I do."

Meyani followed the motion, popping her wrist at the same time Jarrah did but then letting go and bumping the wood as her hand dropped away. The boomerang flew a few feet and dropped.

"You almost had it," Jarrah said as he retrieved it. "Let's try again."

Meyani and Jarrah went through the steps again. The boomerang spun and flew high, only to disappear in a shimmer of light.

"That's weird," Jarrah said. "I'll find it."

Meyani stood rooted in place for a moment and then realized that the boomerang had opened the door – just as the older woman had said. She watched in horror as Jarrah ran toward the opening and disappeared.

She ran.

Holding her breath, she hoped she wouldn't be too late.

Racing forward, she saw a sliver of a brightly lighted door.

She almost slid, trying to duck inside. As she moved through, she felt a rush of wind - the door closing.

She turned around and wobbled on the rock she was standing on. No longer was she on the flat ground outside the cultural center. Instead, she was on the top of a rocky mound as much as she could tell. She hesitated to move and instead tried to get her bearings.

The sun was beating down, and there was a slight wind that gave Meyani a brief respite from the heat. A haze had settled over the area, so Meyani could not see anything clearly. A dark shape moved in her direction, and Meyani began to check the ground, finding a path to move away and down. Each time she moved; the shape changed direction.

As Meyani found her way to the ground, the haze cleared enough for her to see the older woman from the cultural center nearing her. She almost burst into tears of relief that it was a familiar face.

"I wasn't sure what you were. I came through the doorway just as you said, but then it was hazy…"

The woman was frowning.

"Jarrah came through with you. It was not his time. Nor were you to come through at that place. The journey was yours to take alone. Later."

Meyani clutched one arm.

"He was helping me learn to throw the boomerang. I had no idea it would work so quickly."

The woman seemed to consider her words.

"Did you ask for help, or did he offer?"

"He offered."

The older woman looked around as if searching for something.

"The song lines work as they will. You are in one instead of simply observing one from a different vantage. Jarrah is the one observing, although that may change or his time may come later. Now, I am not sure why he is here and you are within. As he is younger, I must help him first. I am sorry, I had hoped to be able to guide you. But you will be alone on your journey through the lines."

The woman turned and began to walk away.

"Wait. I don't know what I am doing or where to go."

"The lines will show you. Just remember you are within the song lines," the woman said.

Meyani looked around. The stones were familiar. She'd been with a small tour that had heard the story of three young girls and mischievous god the day before. Was she back in that place, or was her memory playing tricks on her?

Could this be one of the Aboriginal walking routes that crossed Australia, linking the important sites and locations? She recognized a few features she'd seen in the tour. Was she supposed to find a route to her destination? Or find some wisdom or knowledge from an ancestral spirit?

She moved to her left and found the jagged stone jutting from the ground and the small protected area where the girls in the story had been eating at midday. She could smell the fruity aroma of a spicy riberry with a hint of clove and cinnamon. As she stood there staring, the haze returned, bringing with it the silhouettes of seven young women. She could not see them well.

She heard a cracking behind her.

Meyani turned and saw a green fig tree full of fruit where there had been none.

Behind her, a woman scampered away. Meyani followed.

The women entered a cave opening within the rocky mount that Meyani had climbed down from. Meyani looked back to see the green fig tree transform into a large black snake slithering in the dusty ground.

The shapeshifter from the story she'd heard the day before. He was pursuing the young women.

Meyani ran into the cave, barely seeing the women in the shadows.

"Quick hide, or he will find us."

Meyani looked around to see who they were talking to.

"You. He must not find you, or he will get us all."

Meyani searched for a shadow or indention that would conceal her, but they were all taken by the seven sisters.

"There's nowhere to hide. What should I do?"

One sister spoke up.

"Here, hide by me. I think it's big enough."

Meyani tried to squeeze beside her, but the area was too small. She looked around again.

Nothing.

"Wait. In the story, don't you slip out through a hole at the other end of the cave? Can't I go through that?"

The sisters shook their heads.

"There's not enough time. He would see you and follow you. You could be hurt."

Meyani shook her head.

"I am the one putting you in danger. I will go quickly, and if he sees me, then that is mine to deal with."

Meyani raced to the back of the cave, feeling her way along the wall until she came to the hole. She slipped in head first and began to pull/push her way through as quietly as she could.

At the sound of hissing, she gave one last hard push to the outside.

The opening led her to a small flat area with one side blocked by the rocks. Climbing them or the face of the hill above the hole would be treacherous. Ahead of Meyani, the rocks dropped off, making a descent impossible. Her only option was a small path that led down the front of the rocky mound near where she'd first seen the woman.

She placed one foot gingerly on the rocky path, knowing that the snake could slide down faster than she could walk. She continued, not looking back, hoping that the snake was still inside and the women were safe.

At the bottom of the path, she took two deep breaths and looked back. Shining yellow eyes watched her from above.

Meyani began to run down the path. It was straighter here and more familiar. She passed the fork where the aboriginal boys would meet to learn the ways of being a man. For a second, she considered turning off to throw off the snake in case it followed her.

What if going there was a desecration in the song line? She continued forward to where she'd been shown the women's area the day before. The snake might be prohibited from going there, although she wasn't sure.

Meyani stopped as sweat poured down her back and her breathing became labored. She needed a brief rest in the heat before she continued.

She listened for the snake but heard nothing.

She took a few steps forward, slower now as she tried to keep saliva in her dry mouth. Ahead she heard women speaking and hurried forward.

Under an overhang of rocks, four dark-skinned women with gray and black curly short curly hair betraying their age sat in a semi-circle. One sang while the others were hard at work, making small hand tools and attaching animal pelts together for some garment.

Meyani stepped forward into the clearing before them, not wanting to disturb them and unsure if she would be welcomed.

The singing woman motioned her forward with one hand. She indicated for Meyani to sit in the open space. Meyani sank to the ground thankfully, her legs crossed in front of her to match the other women. The coolness of the ground raised goosebumps on her legs and was a relief to her warm skin.

As the woman finished the song, she said, "You have come a long way."

"You speak English?" Meyani asked.

"Here, all languages exist as one. You have nothing to fear from the snake while you remain with us."

Meyani couldn't quite wrap her brain around that but was relieved that there was someone she could ask questions of.

"Do you know why I am here? In this place? I know I am here to learn something, but it is so confusing. I don't know where to start."

The woman laughed.

"You already have. Entering the song lines is easy for one with our blood in your veins. No matter how little – even a drop will be recognized by that which allows you to enter. The door opens. Being worthy of the knowledge is more difficult, but you showed you were willing to help the seven sisters and put yourself at risk instead of endangering them."

The woman allowed her words to sink in.

"Your life is changing."

Meyani sucked in a breath.

"How did you know I am to marry?"

All the women began to laugh.

"Do not be offended. It is just that what you think is important is of no consequence to us. We are referring to the babe that you will bring into the world. You must protect it from all within the song lines that would do it harm. Remember the shapeshifter? That is only one such as is along the lines. In this life and others."

Meyani leaned forward.

"But I don't know that I can have children. Or how to protect one if I do. Or even what to protect against."

The woman's words were overwhelming to Meyani. Having children was in the future. A distant future at best. This woman spoke as if it was a sure thing that would be happening soon. She looked up and saw the woman's eyes were shining.

"A child is something to cherish, not fear. We will teach you a lullaby which you should sing to your child when they are hurt or lonely or need comfort."

The other women dropped what they were working on and picked up sticks by their sides. They began to beat them against rocks, in time with each other as the singer began.

The words meant nothing to Meyani, who started to hum along and then began to sing as she mastered the sounds for the words. They continued until the singer was satisfied.

"What does the song mean?

"The story is of a young child pursued by a bad spirit who is protected by a beautiful purple butterfly. Can you sing it alone?"

The singer nodded as Meyani started, joining in when she faltered on the words.

"Good. Again. You must take this with you when you leave."

Meyani practiced the song through the afternoon, stopping to drink water a few times. She borrowed the sticks of one woman to help her keep the rhythm as she sang.

At first, the words made no sense, but as she continued singing, images of a young child in danger rose in her mind along with the spirit and the butterfly. At the point where she could not separate the images from the sounds she was singing, the woman smiled.

"You have done well. Take the song with you. It will also keep you safe and comfort you in times of trouble."

Meyani felt better. She was calmer than she'd been in months. She wasn't sure if it was the women or the song or simply sitting in this place with rocks and nature all around.

She felt a cramp in her leg and rose to walk it off. As she turned back, she realized the area had gone quiet. Looking back at where she had been sitting, the area was empty. She was on her own again.

Meyani's heart sank. She had liked the women and the camaraderie of doing things together, something she didn't have at home. Maybe there was something in the ways of these people that she could use.

She looked at the path and decided she'd walk back to the rocky mound. If she'd entered that way, perhaps she could exit that way too. She began to hum the song she'd just learned.

At the base of the mound, she turned right to find a small, almost pathway that looked to take her to the top. Could it be that easy?

She put one foot in front of the other, trudging upwards.

The sounds of rocks sliding and distant footsteps made her stop and turn her head.

Jarrah!

Where had he come from?

He had a welcoming smile on his face.

"Meyani. Wait for me."

She took two steps forward to a place where the rocks were flat, and she could stand. As Jarrah approached, she asked, "Where have you been? Are you okay?"

"Yes, I have had the most wonderful adventure."

Meyani smiled.

"So have I, but now it is time to leave. I'm sorry I can't stay here to talk to you more."

Jarrah looked at her strangely.

"That is why I am here. We came in together and must leave the same way."

Meyani stared at the young man. Something seemed different.

"Let's walk."

Jarrah nodded and stepped forward. Meyani took a step backward, slipped and caught herself. She stared at the ground.

Her shadow was there but Jarrah had none. She looked up to see a wide grin.

"You cannot escape me that easily," the shapeshifter said as it transformed into a snake.

Meyani looked around. There was brush and a few rocks, but nothing that would work as weapon. She turned to run, but also began to hum the song she'd just learned.

A wisp of air made her look up – a purple butterfly was sailing overhead. It dropped a short staff of wood, which Meyani struggled to catch, but missed.

Her eyes met the snakes as she feinted as if she was reaching for the stick. Instead, she stood up straight as the snake struck, missing Meyani.

Meyani reached down and grabbed the stick as the snake tried to react. She hit it in several places and hit the dirt, raising dust that made it hard to see.

Each time she landed a blow, the snake's body was crushed and dissolved where she had hit it.

The snake screamed words in a language Meyani did not understand. It gathered its pieces together in its mouth and retreated down the path.

Meyani stared to follow but stopped short at the sight of Jarrah. Or was it another of the shapeshifter's tricks?

"Meyani? Are you okay? What were you fighting?"

The young man came close to her and she backed up a few steps.

"What were you doing when we met? Meyani asked.

She was almost certain the shapeshifter could not know what had happened on the other side of the portal door. At least she hoped not.

"I was kicking a ball with my friends. Why, what has happened?"

Meyani sighed with relief.

"It is a long story. I think it is time to leave."

"Yes, that is why I was looking for you. Are you ready?"

"Yes. We go to the top?"

Jarrah nodded.

They walked in silence until they reached the top, which flattened out so that they could both stand side by side.

"Hold your hands up. We must catch it together for the opening to come."

Meyani had been wondering how she'd catch the boomerang since they'd never practiced that part. She looked at Jarrah's arms and hands and moved her into the same position near his.

"How will we do this?"

"We will manage. It will return quickly and be moving fast. Just slap your hands together, and we'll be able to grab it."

The words were barely out of his mouth before Meyani heard the whirling of the boomerang. As Jarrah had said, she didn't have time to think, only to move her hands. The two caught the piece of wood together, stepping backward in the awkward stance.

Meyani felt herself falling and reached down one hand to catch herself. As she fell, her hand landed on the green grass in the sandy area where she learned how to throw. Jarrah danced around her, kicking up dust as he tried not to fall on her. He offered her a hand to stand up.

"Are you all right?"

Meyani nodded, thankful that they were back where she had started.

Jarrah was still holding the boomerang and handed it back to her. She ran her fingers over the smooth wood, still amazed at its power. Had this all really happened? Meyani looked up to see Jarrah beaming at her.

"Thank you for teaching me how to throw this. I think I'll find another to take home with me."

Jarrah cocked his head, a question on his face.

"I was told that the boomerang was to be left to find its way home once I was back. I think leaving it with you makes sense. Do you know what to do with it?"

Jarrah smiled.

"I do. The Dreaming is personal, and we don't talk about it. But ours was linked together somehow. Would you like to talk about it?"

Meyani considered the question. It was a personal experience, but she wondered what Jarrah had learned and whether the older woman from the cultural center had found him.

"I would like to talk about it generally. I think what I

learned is personal. And is for you too. Is that something we could do?"

Jarrah nodded.

"First, I need to go inside and get some water. I feel like I could drink several bottles. Do you want some?"

"Yes. I'll wait for you on the bench where you were sitting before. We can rest and talk about what the path was for each of us."

Meyani hurried inside, as much for the cool water as the need to return to the bench and hear about what Jarrah had seen and done. A few members of the tour were still milling around and she wondered how that could be. Time seemed to have stood still while she was gone.

She wasn't sure what the experience meant for her life but she was grateful to the women and the purple butterfly. If she did have a child in the future, she knew that a purple butterfly would always have a place in her home.

PORTAL CENTRAL

Benzer fairly ran down the white hall devoid of any pictures or decoration. The division had only recently been relocated to the larger facility and no one had had time to do anything that wasn't essential to its operation.

The walkway, which was more like a long cave entrance with its narrowness and the curved arch overhead. It ran along the outside wall of the large open area filled with clear conical cubicle areas where he and the other "magicals" worked in.

Although calling Benzer magical was only accurate in the loosest sense of the word. He was one step below Mr. Farajak, his boss, in terms of magic in his blood, which of course, was normal since he was mostly human and it was why he was hired. The head guy couldn't have the least amount of magic in his blood. It just wasn't done.

He shivered as much from the red button on his communication device going off – and meaning that Mr. Farajak wanted to see him – as from the cold, dry air that flowed through the area. Mr. F, as everyone called him outside of his hearing, forbid any food or drink in the work environment so that it remained pristine. How that was supposed to happen with the variety of creatures, from wolf derivations to the fairies that left dust and wafts of perfumed flowers everywhere, was beyond Benzer's comprehension.

The door at the end of the hall loomed large as Benzer moved closer, an optical illusion rather than real magic, but it served its purpose. The words "Jorges Farajak" which could be read at a distance, told him he was at the right place.

Nothing else. No Executive Director. No Head of Portal Central.

Just his name. It was hard to be head of or executive director of something where your powers were different from most of those you oversaw.

At least in the magical world.

Benzer knocked on the door even though he was expected. He was polite above all else.

"Enter."

He stepped into a smallish, hut-like room lined with screens Benzer knew monitored the portal system that Mr. Farajak had built. Benzer stepped back to allow his eyes to refocus and adjust to the constant movement inside. Mr. F sat in the middle, in a low chair that leaned back so that he could view the arched ceiling as well as the walls, his round head twisting this way and that as he watched. A dash of white here and there told Benzer that the walls were the same colors as the hall, only wholly covered here where the outside had been bare.

In the cubicle area Benzer had just left, there were similar monitors but no more than two or three per employee to make sure nothing out of the ordinary, operationally, was missed. Benzer only had one monitor since it was assumed he could only do one thing at a time, a perception he'd cultivated. The cubicle system mimicked the primary portal system so that the workers had a sense of the entire system simply by working within it.

As he sat on the perch he'd been given in his cubby hole in the room's far corner, he'd watched how the ghosts levitated, the fairies flew and floated, and how the trolls hoarded things that they treasured, capturing the concepts and adjusting them to fit within his limited magical abilities. All the while increasing the strength of what he had, without displaying any of his newfound abilities.

Benzer's screen had been set up to watch a mostly unused portal. The system was a pattern of gateways that anyone could use – magical or not. They were set in place with doors that could be accessed in various ways, depending on the skills of the party seeking to enter. The exits were set in place as well. Something like the old train or bus stations that he'd experienced in his human home world. They didn't replace the personal and private portals that many had or the many other portals between worlds. Rather, the system was to begin to put in place portals that were streamlined and didn't overlap other portals which could result in those traveling through them arriving in unexpected places.

He'd synced his monitor to notify him on his communication device when there was movement. A small vibration on his wrist alerted him, the normal level he expected, except for this morning when the red button had sent a jolt up his arm. He'd almost fallen off his perch as he leaped to his feet.

Now, standing before the other human in the complex, Benzer had recovered from the shock of the call and wondered why he'd been summoned.

"Benzer, stop your daydreaming. Your help is needed."

Benzer swung his head back to face the man who now stood before him. They were about the same height and weight. They both had brown hair and faces that were ordinary. Like they both could melt into a crowd.

"Yes, sir. You sent for me."

Mr. F frowned.

"We have three portals which are not working properly. I can't investigate them myself since I need to be here, but you can."

Benzer looked around for some kind of escape or reasoning that could free him.

"You are the engineer that designed this system. I'm just a techie. How can I help?"

Mr. F laughed.

"You are more than that. You have been learning about the creatures here, their abilities, and this system all the time you have been here. If it weren't that I knew your parents, I'd think you were an industrial portal spy out to steal the secrets of how this works."

Benzer started to protest.

"No, I had you checked out. And I've been personally watching you. You are more than meets the eye, although no one I have talked to seems to think so. You've hidden your interest very well."

Benzer kept his eyes forward, commanding his body to stay still and not give away the fear he felt. A shiver ran down his back as the cold air began to churn in the room. While his stomach churned, his blood quickened at the thought of the challenge being offered to him.

"What do you want me to do?"

"Now there's the spirit. I want you to investigate what is happening at the portals in the system. Ignore all the personal ones that you run across. I am only interested in the ones within the system. We need to know if they are being tampered with or sabotaged."

Benzer sucked in a breath and then regretted it as his mouth went dry.

"I don't know anything about investigating something like this."

Mr. F's smile deepened.

"But you did take a correspondence course on crime investigation, didn't you?"

Benzer could feel the heat on his face. No one was supposed to know about that. He'd been interested in the subject, hoping but never dreaming he might actually use it.

"Yes, but that was a long time ago, and I've never used anything I learned."

"Think of it as your background for this. It's just three portals, and you should be able to go to each one, observe the area, the entrances and the exits. Then, come back to report.

You are not to tell anyone you are doing this, and you answer only to me."

Benzer nodded.

"I'll do the best I can, but I don't know how I'll know if a magical has tampered with it."

Mr. F grinned.

"That's something I can help with. I not only invented this system, but I have a few gadgets I've created in the past few years that will help you. Let's go into my laboratory."

Mr. F moved to one wall, laid a hand about two feet higher than his shoulder on it, then a quick slap and a pop, and he opened up what looked to be a large closet. Until Benzer stepped inside, and it became a room larger than the one they had been in.

"You're not to tell anyone about this either. This portal is not on the main system and is for my private use."

Benzer's eyes widen as he took in the contents. One wall was covered in weapons of all sizes and shapes that he could hardly contemplate what beings or circumstances they were used for. Another wall had body armor that ranged from historic chainmail to plastics to other materials that glistened as if wet to the touch.

"Over here," Mr. F said as he rummaged through one section. "You'll need this and this, and maybe this."

Mr. F turned around and led the way back out, putting his hand on a hidden pad that opened the wall again. He checked to make sure no one had entered his office before he walked over to his chair and set the items on it.

"Let's run through these. This is a detector of magic that has compartments for specimens to hold what you find."

Benzer was staring at the wall, trying to see where the portal door was.

"You can stop that. The portal moves each time. Only I know where it will be next."

Benzer turned around.

"Here. See the black button on top? Push it."

The little black box was almost weightless and fit in Benzer's palm. He pushed the button and almost dropped the tool. Instead of a square thin wafer-like piece, it transformed into a long cylindrical hose with a handle.

"You push the side button and it will extract anything, including magic. You'll know it has found something when whatever it vacuums in turns to silver. You can return it to the original shape by pushing the button on top a second time. Be careful that you have obtained everything you need so that it goes into the retainer section. Each time you extract something new, it will assign it to a new section. That way, we'll know where the material came from. Got it?"

Benzer nodded, although he wasn't at all sure he had anything.

Mr. F loaded the black box into a black fabric carrying case which he picked up from beside his chair. He lifted a new item – a circular compact. He clicked it open and demonstrated how it worked.

"This will get you to each portal entrance, through it, and then back to the same point again. I've programmed in each coordinate for the entry and exit since they are in the stable portal system. You shouldn't have any problems.

Benzer wanted to ask him to repeat the instructions, but Mr. F had already moved on.

"I don't think you'll need it, but in case you are discovered, you only have to say the word "jumper" as you hold this in your right hand. That will bring you back here if there's trouble. Don't use it unless you must since whoever is there will realize you aren't me."

Benzer watched as the object went into the bag.

"The most important item I have for you is a duplicate of my pass. It will let you into anywhere in the complex. Since we are similar in build, no one should question you, but if someone does, just glare at them and keep moving. You are better off if no one takes too close a look."

"But what if…"

"No delay now. The faster we know what is going on, the sooner we can resolve this. Besides, almost no one uses these three portals, so you shouldn't encounter anyone."

Benzer wasn't so sure that would be the case, but his thoughts were flying faster than a genie set free from a bottle after three hundred years.

"Don't I need a weapon? What if someone stops me or discovers I am not you?"

Mr. F puffed up his chest.

"A weapon? Good grief, no. This is not some secret spy mission. You are on a quest for the information we need. Don't even think about it. And if you get caught, you're on your own unless you pull the emergency mechanism."

Mr. F waited for a response, and when Benzer said nothing, he continued.

"I'm depending on you. I know you can do this and be stealthy about it. It would upset the entire program if word got out."

Benzer was about to answer when the door flew open.

"Jorges, what is going on. I hear rumors the portal system has problems."

Mr. F waved Benzer off as he turned.

"Andreas, you worry too much. A slight issue. I already have beings working on solutions."

"I vouched for you. If it doesn't work, it reflects badly on me. That's not…"

Benzer picked up the bag, slipped by Andrea and closed the door behind him, all the while wondering how bad things really were if Mr. F's brother was paying him a personal visit. He would have loved to stay and try to eavesdrop, but although the hall was empty, there was no place to hide if anyone approached.

Andreas was a magical of the first order and a member of the Council that helped maintain some kind of arrangement between the species. That alone made Benzer pause and think through what he was about to do. Plus, he suspected others were working on the same problem.

His investigations class had promoted caution and surveillance before entering any new area or structure. Benzer headed back to his cubicle. He stepped up his pace. He needed a few things, and he wanted to check the layout for the locations he'd need to transport to.

Benzer looked around the room as he transferred the items Mr. F had given him to his brown leather backpack. No one paid him any attention on any given day, so his long stare at certain locations went unnoticed. Or at least he hoped so.

Mr. F had told him to start immediately, but if he left early, it could be noticed. So he spent his time contacting two friends, Erdich and Robards. They had more magic and had been willing to help Benzer in his practice to increase his magic.

One time measure later, and Benzer left. He had a whole story of why he was leaving early, but no one noticed or questioned him. Instead, he walked out as if he was invisible, which was just fine with him.

He lengthened his stride to arrive at the corner of the corridor that intersected with another, marking the turn he had to make to reach the first portal entrance. As Benzer had suspected, when he walked by the corridor and looked to its end, there were creatures there. Three dwarves were working on the portal entrance.

The short, husky dwarves were employed for the actual repairs of the system. They had no magic nor the ability to register magic, and could be difficult to deal with.

He silently cursed Mr. F and wondered if he was being set

up. It was possible. Or it might be a test. Either way, Erdich's and Robards' help was needed for a distraction.

As he reached the other side of the corridor, Benzer noted the two sauntering toward him. He quickly explained his plan, and they agreed.

The two were wider and taller than Benzer, making it easy for him to slip behind them unnoticed as they headed toward the portal.

"Got any big plans for your time off?" Erdich asked as he punched Robards in the shoulder.

"Better than yours," Robards laughed as he punched back, his hand slipping and catching Erdich on his chin.

"Hey, you did that on purpose."

Erdich shoved Robards so that he bounced off the side wall. Benzer scooted behind Erdich as much as possible so the dwarves would not see him.

The two kept the scuffle up until they were in front of the workers.

One of the dwarves looked to be in charge and turned to grunt at them.

"You can't go through here. The portals stuck. Go to another one."

"We don't want another one," Erdich said. "Get out of our way."

The dwarf frowned and put his hands on his hips.

"You don't want to mess with me. Go away."

Robards laughed.

"No. Make me."

The other two dwarves dropped their tools and turned to face them. Erdich moved to one side to shield Benzer, who had already pulled out his device, a magic detector which registered who had last used magic there.

He didn't see any residual that he could vacuum up, but he'd have to do that when the dwarves weren't around. He pocketed the device for the moment. In its place, he opened the compact and dialed in the exit on the portal.

Robards and Erdich leaped forward, punching at all three dwarves. Benzer hoped the three workers hadn't seen him, but he wouldn't know for sure until he returned.

Benzer hit the button to go through the portal, which opened with a flash and closed as quickly as he stepped through. He hadn't been sure it would open at all, but Mr. F had assured him the compact would override any other magic that had disabled this system gateway.

On the other side, Benzer breathed in, relaxing his shoulders, when he saw that he was alone. He hadn't been sure he'd be able to pull off the stun, even with this friends' help.

Benzer pulled out the square box and pushed the button so the vacuum hose extended. He eased the end around where the portal had been. Bits and fragments of a silvery substance were drawn in. When he finished the door, he ran it along the white floor in front of the portal and picked up some shiny blue material as well.

It could be simple organic material or something he hadn't ever encountered. Benzer turned off the vacuum, hit the switch to return it to the palm-size box, and replaced it in his backpack. It was time to return.

Benzer dialed the compact and waited.

No response.

Which was weird. Mr. F hadn't said anything about having to use things in a particular order or not being able to return somewhere. Maybe the system was actually broken.

Benzer tried using Mr. F's override pass card.

No response. Again, either Mr. F was testing him, or it was defective, or, and he didn't want to think about this one, Mr. F was in trouble which meant visiting the other portals might be risky.

Benzer considered his options. He could stay where he was

and keep trying or move on, knowing he could return to the first portal spot later by another method.

He decided to move on. Having been successful on the first portal, he sent a quick message on his communicator device to Erdich and Robards to meet him at the third portal. He'd handle the second one on his own - an outer point of the system and rarely used. The chances anyone was there were slim, and he'd be in and out quickly.

He set the compact for a portal need where his second target existed.

"You there. What are you doing here? Don't you know this is a restricted area?"

Benzer turned to see a dragon guard standing on his hind legs before him. A small dragon, but a fire-eating one that could take him out with one swipe of his muscular green arm.

He fought with his quivering legs to keep himself upright. The security ones had no sense of humor and were strict about the rules.

"I'm lost. I was supposed to find Hogging Den portal to visit my friend, according to his directions."

The dragon seemed to relax a bit.

"That's down the next corridor. Go now, or I'll have to cite you for this."

"Yes, sir," Benzer said, glad he'd taken the time to learn the entire system and all the stop names. The class about doing your homework on surveillance and background information had paid off. He moved forward, glancing around and trying to determine why this spot might be guarded but found no clues.

Benzer stepped carefully over the dragon's tail and skipped to the end of the corridor, turned right, and hung on the outskirts of a group of grubby trolls complaining about the working conditions of one passageway they were building nearby. Benzer milled about like a few other human creatures waiting to enter various hallways. He edged himself to the opposite wall, feeling as if the dragon might be still watching him.

He slipped around a corner to a quieter and empty area, pushed the button, and hoped the second portal wasn't guarded.

The corridor was empty when Benzer arrived. A large red sign stated, "Portal Not in Use."

All was quiet, almost too quiet. The hairs on the back of his neck stood up. Was there a watchdog of some sort? Or an electronic surveillance?

Benzer reached out with his limited magical abilities but detected nothing unusual. He moved his head. Then back again. Something was in the corner. A slight flash his peripherical sight had noted. Most would not have seen it, but Benzer's eyes took in a broader scan than most creatures. Sometimes there was something there and others not. Here, he didn't dare ignore it.

He stepped to one side.

Nothing sounded.

He stepped to the other side.

Again, nothing.

He took a step back.

Nothing.

Benzer swung his backpack around and reached inside. He'd scored some fairy dust which he planned to use to try out flying. It couldn't be helped – it was needed now. Benzer lifted the transparent container and opened the lid.

He swung the box so that the dust flew high away from him and trickled down, lighting up the cross-hatched section of red lights. He noted that the strands ran from where his knees were up to his throat.

He'd been right. If he'd stepped forward, alarms would have gone off.

The question was, should he go over or under?

Benzer dropped the backpack and patted it down so that it was as compact as possible. He took one more look and gave it a hard push, sliding it across the floor until it smacked into the wall across from him.

His heart raced. He'd solved at least that part. Now, he just needed to get across.

He could crawl, but he might singe his elbows or worse. Or he could scoop up the fairy dust from the floor and try to fly.

He had it on good authority that it only took a small amount sprinkled over his head, and he could fly for an hour or more. Benzer didn't need that, but experimenting here was risky.

He grinned. What was life without a bit of fun?

Benzer gathered up the dust and dropped some on his head. It tickled his nose and made his hands itch, but he felt lighter.

His feet rose off the floor and he tried maneuvering. Awkward, as he twisted, then an arm would drop or his leg dangled. He'd need full control to get to where he was going.

He willed himself higher, bumping into the ceiling.

He flattened his body out, but his head was facing the wrong way. He turned.

Using a swimming motion with his arms, he felt the air swirl by him as he propelled forward.

His blood raced. He was flying.

Headed straight into a fairy, who twinkled in brightness. Benzer realized that having a lookout might have been smarter than going it alone.

"Unauthorized flying is a magical offense," the fairy said, her arms on her tiny hips as she hovered in front of him.

"Umm. Sorry. A friend gave me some to try out and I couldn't wait."

"Get down now. Be careful of the lasers, or you'll set off the alarms, which will mean even more offenses. You're lucky the dust set off an alarm for me and not one of the dragons."

"Can you help me with that? I've never flown before."

The fairy scoffed.

"Just aim for the floor and think down."

Benzer did as he was told and found himself crashing into the hard floor face first, although his arms took the brunt of the landing. He jerked his feet in and leaned against the wall.

"Identification, please."

Benzer reached inside the backpack and felt around. The pass card fell out, and the fairy swooped over to grab it before he could check it.

"Mr. Farajak."

The fairy's eyes grew rounder and more prominent.

"Oh sir, I am so sorry. I didn't recognize you. Your picture doesn't look exactly like you either."

Benzer almost laughed.

"It is an old one. We humans change over time. Did you know that?"

The fairy seemed unconvinced but then shrugged.

"I hadn't, but I am glad to know that. I hope I didn't inconvenience you."

"No, you were just doing your job. I guess you found me out. I was given the fairy dust so I could try out the alarm system. Find the vulnerabilities. As you can see, we need to strengthen this one. However, I am glad to see the fairies are on the job. I'll have to commend you to your supervisor, Fairy ..."

The fairy puffed out her chest.

"I'm Mathilde, sir. I'd be very appreciative if you put in a good word for me."

"No problem. I'll do that when I am back in my office. Now, I need to finish my examination here."

The fairy moved back a bit.

"You haven't ever seen silvery blue magic, have you? Someone mentioned that the other day."

"Blue silver is very bad, sir. Very bad. It means that a magical is turning toward the dark side of magic but is not yet fully there. I'd avoid that if I was you."

Benzer smiled.

"I owe you again. Now, I need to get back to work."

"Of course, I'll leave you here, sir. Good luck."

Benzer smiled. The fairy would be disappointed, but he'd see if he could find a way to make things right since he had promised her. The blue silver was troubling. Mr. F might have found a way to increase his magic by the black arts. Or someone else could be involved.

She disappeared in a poof.

Benzer pulled out the vacuum square and opened it. He repeated the process of scooping up the silvery substance. On the floor, he ran over it again but only found more silver. He closed it so that the material went into the reserve compartment.

Using the compact, the portal opened, and Benzer found himself on the other side. Once again, he used the vacuum to recover more silver.

Something was off, but he couldn't seem to focus on it. Then it hit him. Why all the security on the other side if this wasn't a critical portal? Was it protecting against an intruder or an early warning for whoever had damaged the portals? Who would have that kind of access? Only a few people. Mr. F, Benzer's supervisor who ran the cubicle and the Council.

Was Mr. F's brother behind this? Or Mr. F? Or both of them? Nothing made sense. The portal system was mainly for humans with lesser magical ability. What did either of them gain from sabotaging things or being able to manipulate it? Or was Benzer being set up for a system that had a fundamental problem?

Benzer let the thoughts bounce around. He would go to the third portal and gather more evidence. Then he'd use some time to think things through. First though, he had an idea that he needed to protect himself.

There were small shops with containers in the back where one could store valuables or items for a short time. One Benzer had used before was two stops before the third portal. He used his own identity card and entered a central portal that let him out near where he'd been before.

He used the stroll, checking out corridors, to see if anything looked unusual. When he found nothing out of the ordinary, he entered the shop, nodded to the owner who was with a customer. The store was long and narrow, with a long bar on one side in front of jars of creams and herbal remedies. On the opposite wall were bins of cookware and cleaning materials.

Rows of stacked containers were along the back wall. They varied in size, but the open ones were clear while the ones that contained contents were black.

Benzer waited until the owner was free.

"I need to drain a bit of material from each of the segments within this. Can you do that?" Benzer asked.

The owner eyed the vacuum contraption that Benzer revealed and without a word, moved to close the shop door, turning his closed sign on.

"Where did you get that thing?"

Benzer winced at the sharp tone. The man was his cousin and always seemed to be angry at the world.

"I can't say. The less you know, the better. Can you do it?"

The man rolled his eyes.

"Of course, but this one is going to cost you. How much should I take?"

"No more than a drop or two. Leave some of each one. I need them in separate containers and marked."

The man turned and headed to the back of the store.

"Bring it. I'll retrieve the material. You mark it. Put it into your container when we're done."

Benzer carefully marked the tubes as the man added some liquid to each one. His investigation class had emphasized having a backup plan, and this was his contingency. He had no idea what was waiting at the third portal and hoped his friends were not in trouble.

Finishing up the last vial, the man capped it and handed it to Benzer.

"Get these put up quickly. I need to open the store again, or there might be questions. A short closure is ordinary, a longer one is not."

Benzer wrote on the last bottle. He opened his container up with his personal keyed password and set them inside. As an afterthought, he also removed Mr. F's pass card and added it to the stash. He'd been considering closing the rental rather than pay the monthly fee since he'd not had anything to keep secure. Now, he was glad he had it.

Walking back through the store, Benzer nodded to the owner and headed out. He found a quiet space as the day shift had left, and the night shift were in their workspaces.

He opened the compact and clicked over to the coordinates. He pushed down, the portal opened, and he entered.

On the other side, two of the dragon guards were waiting. They took his backpack and marched him away. Benzer caught sight of Erdich and Robards, who shrugged their shoulders as if to say they couldn't do anything. He winked, letting them know he understood. As he moved forward, he watched them melt back into the crowd.

Three corridors down, Benzer and his guards were met by Andreas Farajak and Mr. F.

"We'll take him from here," Andreas said as he took the backpack from the dragon holding it. He searched inside and then closed it.

The guards saluted and turned back.

Andreas moved to the sidewall and raised his hand, bringing it down with a slap. A portal opened, and all three walked through.

On the other side was a chamber that Benzer assumed was where the Council met. Raised seats in a semi-circle were filled with six creatures: two dragons, two fairies, a dwarf, and a troll. Andreas moved to take the final seat. Mr. F remained at Benzer's side.

The room was small, considering the creatures in it. Benzer could see no portals or other obvious means to escape. On the walls was a continuing mural reflecting the four seasons commonly seen on Earth as a commentary on time passing. Or maybe it was meant to give him some reference point. Did they do this for each creature that came to stand before the Council? If so, it wasn't working.

Mr. F hadn't said a word or given any indication he knew Benzer. Nor had Andreas, although Benzer wasn't sure Andreas had gotten a good enough look to know he'd been in Mr. F's office earlier.

Benzer could hardly believe how little time had gone by.

Andreas began to speak.

"As you know, we have heard rumors that the portal system has some problems. Several of the standard entrances and exits are not working properly. Can you confirm this, Jorges?"

Benzer stood still, hoping he could fade into the background but feared his time of questioning was coming.

"You know that is true. I told you this in my office earlier when you came to question me. I told you I have dwarves working on several of the stations and that we are working to have them back online shortly," Mr. F said.

"Andreas, if you knew this, why are we here?" asked one of the fairies.

"Because it would appear that there is more to this problem than mechanics," Andreas said.

Andreas lifted the backpack and pulled out the square box. He pushed the button, and the vacuum extended.

"And what is that?" the same fairy asked.

"Jorges, would you care to explain? Or maybe the human?" Andreas asked.

Mr. F remained silent.

Benzer was torn. Was this a power play, or was Mr. F playing some kind of game of control?

"Young man, what is your name?" the fairy asked.

"Benzer."

"Benzer. A strange name, but no matter. Where did you get this, and what is its purpose?"

Benzer stared at the floor, searching for the right answer. One that got him out of his room but left him with a job. Preferably one that didn't anger either of the Farajak men.

"I won it. I know games of chance are frowned upon, but they are fun. It was last night, and while I was able to operate it, I haven't had a chance to check it out further. As you'll see from my record, I like to learn things and explore places."

Benzer could almost feel Mr. F's eyes on him. He ignored the feeling and stared straight ahead at the fairy, who seemed to be fading in and out of view. Strange since the others were solid figures. He wasn't sure if she was a hologram or if her flittering about was causing the effect.

"You won it?" Andreas asked, the scorn in his voice evident. "You expect us to believe you?"

"You can ask my friends who were there. They'll vouch for me."

At least he hoped they would as Benzer turned his head to stare at Andreas.

"This would take an inventor to create, someone with say, an engineering background. Do you have one, Benzer?"

"No."

"Perhaps someone like my brother, Jorges."

"I wouldn't know."

One of the dragons stood and began to pace.

"Do we have a family matter here instead of Council business, Andreas? That would be an abuse of our system."

Andreas paled at the suggestion, and slouched in the chair.

"I am only trying to get to the heart of the matter with the portal system."

The dragon walked in front of Andreas.

"Then how does this tool fit in that discussion?"

Andreas stared at the dragon.

"I don't know, but I will find out."

As the dragon moved to sit on its perch again, Benzer saw Andreas' frown deepen as he stared at his brother. Benzer guessed that Andreas knew that Jorges had made the vacuum he held in his hand. What he didn't know yet was who Benzer was or his role.

"Perhaps we can re-convene when you have more answers?" the fairy said.

Before Andreas could respond, the dragon answered.

"Agreed. All in favor?"

Each of the creatures indicated their approval, except Andreas, whose face suggested he'd like to kill someone.

The creatures rose, and one by one exited via a private portal they initiated. The fairy left last, and Benzer caught a bit of a twinkle on her way out.

Mr. F turned to Benzer and asked, "you work in my department?"

"Yes."

"We'll exit to my office using my pass card. Follow me."

As they turned, Andreas spoke up.

"This isn't over, Jorges. I know you made this instrument. Tell me, what secrets will it reveal when I have it analyzed?"

Andreas turned back.

"I have no idea. I'm sure you'll tell me once you know. After all, we both want the portal system to work, don't we?"

Andreas sighed.

"Power. That's what you want. I want the system for the good of the humans and the other creatures."

"So you say. I'll see you later, brother."

Mr. F initiated the portal, and he and Benzer walked through, entering Mr. F's office.

"Well, that was unpleasant. I thought you'd handle this a bit more circumspect, but I guess it can't be helped. I didn't know my brother was following the repairs so closely."

Mr. F sat down.

"What do you have to report? Did you gather material in the vacuum?"

Benzer nodded.

"I gathered several specimens from the first two portals. Different kinds. One silver and one blue. A bit of other organic material."

Mr. F smiled.

"That's excellent, except that my brother has it. He'll send it to one of his scientist friends to analyze. You'll need to steal it back."

Benzer gasped.

"What? I was just before the Council for what I did for you. How can you ask me to do more?"

"I'm not asking."

Benzer took a step back. He knew that if he refused, he'd make an enemy. If he stole the vacuum, then Andreas would likely know it was him, and he'd make an enemy there too.

"All right. But this is all I will do. Do you know where it will be?"

Mr. F stood and came over to pat Benzer on the shoulder.

"I'll find out. It may take a day or two. I'll contact you."

Mr. F moved back to his chair.

"Also, do you have my duplicate passkey?"

Benzer shook his head.

"It was in my backpack."

Mr. F shrugged.

"I'll have someone get you a new one and destroy the old. We can't have that pass card loose, can we?"

"No, sir."

"You may go."

Benzer walked to the door and then bolted down the corridor. He needed to find Erdich and Robards. There was work to do.

Benzer went back to his cubicle to confirm where the Council had ordered all magicals to provide information on their powers and proof of their white magic source. Benzer had had to do this years ago before he could work at his current position. The information and documentation were still located in the same place.

A quick message to Erdich and Robards to meet at his cousin's store, and Benzer was off with a spare backpack he had. He figured one of the Farajak brothers' magic sources was in the vacuum. All he had to do was match them up, and he'd know who the culprit was. And which one's powers were going dark.

Benzer used the main portal system to arrive near his cousin's store. He explained what had happened to Erdich and Robards after he had left them at the first portal. Erdich was nursing a swollen eye and Robards had a cut lip, but they were both game for helping Benzer determine which of the Farajak brothers' essence was in the vials.

The three headed to the back of the store, which was still open to the public, and Benzer emptied the storage container, adding everything to the backpack.

Back outside, they walked down the corridor to a portal

entrance that would take them back to the second portal. It was blocked, but with Mr. F's pass card, Benzer was able to override the system. They arrived at a dark corridor with no one in sight.

Hurrying forward, they arrived at the laboratory where magical essence is extracted and cataloged. The lab was smaller, with a few offices to one side for the medical technicians. Open areas were divided into compartmental-type sections of white walls that made the place seem like a maze. The place, normally buzzing with activity and conversation, was quiet, making it seem creepier than it was.

All three had been in the lab before for tests at some point, so they were able to locate a room they could use to compare the samples.

Robards found syringes in a drawer, and Benzer connected into the overall technology system using Mr. F's passkey. Erdich took control of the scope that would analyze the liquid. They worked as a team, with Erdich being the more scientific oriented of the three, so he handled the specimens under glass.

They analyzed the liquids twice.

Benzer sat back in a chair, trying to understand.

At the first portal, he'd found silver and blue substances. The silver matched Andreas, and the blue matched Mr. F's. That made a certain kind of sense except that the blue was fainter, which meant that he was moving toward silver more than he was moving toward black.

The organic material didn't match either of the two men.

Benzer leaped up.

"Test the organic material again. There were dwarves working there. Could it be from them?"

Robards added a liquid to one sample and examined it. Benzer compared it to a dwarf's records.

Nothing.

"I saw a dragon at several of these. Could it be something related to a dragon?"

Robards repeated the process, and compared it to a dragon's records.

Nothing.

"Could have told you that wasn't the answer," Erdich said.

"Why?" Benzer asked.

"It smells too sweet to be connected to a dragon or dwarf."

Benzer looked around. He stared at the floor. It was so simple. He couldn't believe it. There was no way the fairy at the second portal had been able to arrive so quickly unless she'd been watching for anyone to be there. And she likely knew Andreas' brother.

"Test for a fairy or fairy dust."

Robards went through the same procedure for a third and fourth time. The comparison with a fairy's record didn't match. But there was fairy dust. Slight and almost undetectable, as if someone had been trying to hide it among another substance.

"Why would the fairies want the system to fail?"

Robards and Erdich stared at Benzer.

"Maybe that's the wrong question," Robards said.

"You mean, the fairies think that Andreas and Mr. F have too much power together? If they separate them and pit them against each other, then they are less able to affect things?"

Robards and Erdich nodded.

"That's pretty cold," Erdich said. "I always liked fairies."

Benzer started to laugh. The other two joined in.

"Let's get this cleaned up. I need to report to Mr. F tomorrow.

The three erased any evidence of their presence. They left through the same portal using Mr. F's pass card to get them into the central system. Robards and Erdich clapped Benzer on the back.

"Pretty good investigating job. Maybe you should start a business and hire us to help you."

Benzer grinned.

"I couldn't have done it without you. I might just have to think about doing something along those lines."

Benzer headed home. He needed some sleep before he faced Mr. F in the morning.

Mr. F might not be too happy he'd used his card and lied about it being in Benzer's backpack, but Benzer figured he could smooth it over. Mr. F might be able to remove the times Benzer had used it to access the places he'd been. Plus, he'd finished his task without stealing the vacuum or backpack from Andreas. Now Mr. F could approach his brother directly.

In any event, Benzer had the proof Mr. F needed to determine his next move in this game of power.

Jennie stepped around the piano, testing the wood plank floor to make sure it would hold her weight. And sneezed.

The force jarred her footing and she heard a deep crack.

She jerked back. Trying again, she found a solid board and moved again. She sighed, as she always did when she was inside the house. Uncle Hugo would have been so terribly sad. She was too.

She'd loved the old house growing up as a kid. Running the curved staircase, hiding in the nooks and crannies of the attic, pretending not to hear her mother calling her to supper. Now the mustiness of the air made it hard to breathe and left a taste of moldy cheese on her tongue.

This time, she took a moment to take it all in. The electricity was out so she could only come during the daytime. If she couldn't find money to make the repairs, the house would have to be sold. And the piano too, since the cost to move it was too great.

The first thing she'd done on entering was to remove the plastic covering over the piano which had been there since her mother had died months before. Pieces of furniture had been removed by family over the years but everyone knew the piano was Jennie's to take. The house had been in disrepair long before Jennie's mother moved in with her sister and had only deteriorated as time went on.

Jennie had spent the last hour tuning the instrument. A task that had been a joy to spend with her uncle, when her mother wasn't around. Each time she worked on the innards of the instrument she could almost feel him looking over her shoulder, even as she listened for her mother's footstep. She'd learned well and picked up extra money doing the same as a freelancer, but it was never enough.

If Uncle Hugo could see the state of his beloved piano and his former home, he'd have condemned and cursed them all. And they deserved it. After all the hours of listening to him play a mix of classical symphonies and ragtime, filling the room with melodies, they'd left that proud instrument to sit and draw dust so that the white keys were almost indistinguishable from the black ones. Bits of dirt littered the top of the piano as if the mice had had a picnic but not cleaned up afterwards.

Tears filled her eyes. She'd tried to take the piano years ago, but her mother had insisted that it remain exactly where Uncle Hugo had left it. And the family had not objected, not outright, choosing to be silent. Just as Uncle Hugo had left them without a word.

Jennie had never learned the reasons for the divide – not even when her mother was on her death bed. She'd cursed Hugo. Condemned him to be tied to "that damned piano" in life and death.

She tiptoed to the side of the upright, as if any noise would bring everything tumbling down. She swiped her hand over the top, feeling the cool smoothness of the polished wood. Clearing a spot so the piano could breathe one final time before it was sold or worse, destroyed. Still elegant beneath the surface dirt accumulated over twenty years.

Jennie lowered her fingers to the piano keys, as if she was reaching out to touch a fine piece of silk. She barely noticed the hardness of the bench where the sheets of music her uncle had collected over the years lived inside.

As she began to play, the winds from a storm brewing set the house to creaking, protesting that its old bones should have to stand against the strength of the new fury.

Jennie played on, the whipping of the force outside disappearing from her ears as she emersed herself within the major and minor scales.

The rain began, softly at first, until it burst into her composition, demanding that the beat of its drumming drive the melody. Once it had established itself, it retreated into the background.

The longer Jennie played, the more the stress of the money needed for the house repairs released. Generations had lived here and now she had to choose between keeping her old home, having a place to live in the city or keeping the piano she'd never dreamed she'd have to sell.

The tunes came easily, one after the other as Jennie was swept deeper and deeper into the music. Her fingers ran the keyboard, into the lower registers on some songs while returning to the upper registers on others.

Old familiar melodies morphed into new sounds and combinations. She slipped into a Scott Joplin ragtime piece with her left-hand jumping to the beat in 4-4 time while her right played a jubilant melody. From there, she slowed into the mournful notes of "Yesterday."

As Jennie shifted into a song reaching the higher register of the notes, lightening stuck sending a brilliant flash of light through the room. Thunder boomed.

Reaching a crescendo of a song, Jennie closed her eyes as she hit the high "C" just as lightning streaked across the sky, hitting a tree in the front of the house with a loud pop. The high "C" note screeched, out of tune, with the music, and there was a smaller pop as if something had broken inside the piano. Jennie clapped her hands over her ears and squeezed her eyes shut, seeking to escape from the discord of the lingering note and the thunderous roar outside.

As she did, the world seemed to right itself with the noise gone.

Jennie opened her eyes.

The house and its walls had vanished. The piano was gone.

The wind remained and gray and black clouds swirled, bringing with them more rain, reaching down to the water creating a type of tunnel with no end.

She hadn't realized she had stood up, but was now balanced on one end of a large keyboard with white and black keys in an open sea of yellowish, writhing water. The tide was coming in and covering the keys. The water lapped at her tennis shoes and she could feel the cold wetness as it seeped inside. The seawater carried a stale, sulphury smell that lingered in her nose.

Jennie moved forward, each key giving off its sound as if she was walking on a giant piano keyboard. She glanced back, seeing the water begin to wash over where she had just been standing.

She hurried.

Ahead of her she could see a sandy beach with a rocky hill within feet of it. If she didn't want to swim, she'd need to run. A few breaks in the water marked the fins of creatures below that were yet unseen. Even more reason to be on the land.

Faster and faster, she balanced on the two-foot-wide planks under her feet.

Crashing waves, sent droplets of moisture that added to the slickness of the polished wood.

Her hands flew up to try to regain her balance as one foot slipped. Moving forward a bit more carefully, she focused on one foot in front of the other until she took a final leap over the last two keys to land on the beach.

One foot sank into the sand and she jerked it free.

Scanning the area, she tentatively put pressure on a black rock.

It held.

There was a line of rocks to the cliff side. No sign of a trail.

Jennie would deal with the rocks first since the water was creeping closer.

The rocks were jagged with some flat areas. Jennie's back was soaked in sweat and her breath ragged from exertion. She settled her toes on each rock before bringing down a heel, keeping her other foot firmly on the rock she had already tested.

One by one, she made her way to the cliff.

As she stepped onto the last stone, a boulder stood before her.

She climbed on top, taking a moment to breathe as she escaped the water inching towards her. From her viewpoint, she could see the beginnings of a trail leading out of the weather.

The tide was still coming in and being sucked into the water behind her was not an option.

Jennie started up the path.

It was part sand and part rock, with bits and pieces set free with each step she took. Overgrown brown brush that looked more dead than alive grabbed at her jeans as she moved past.

She stopped to look back, then wished she hadn't.

The water hadn't completely reclaimed the piano key route she'd followed, but neither had it receded. Both ends were submerged. Would it be there if she tried to go back? Jennie didn't want to think about the answer to that question or having to swim out to climb onto the wobbly bridge.

She squared her shoulders and took two deep breaths. The land trail had taken her toward the lower side of the hill before turning up. She was close to reaching the top.

Walking carefully, Jennie reached the summit of the trail and looked around.

The path continued on a downward angle to a gate. With a guard house. Where was she?

With no way back that seemed certain, she moved forward.

Approaching the gate, she saw that it was of an iron alloy, much like something she would see in a gated community. Curlicues within each side of the gate roamed through with intermittent solid circles before the two sides joined in the middle – locked and closed to outsiders. The name at the top on each side read "Discordia."

She walked a few more steps. Beside the gate was a small house like structure that she guessed was a guard house. A small door was marked by a similarly curved knocker which she used to announce her presence.

The wooden door opened. A massive door, twice her height and as thick as a ceiling beam that supported a house. What lived nearby that would require the kind of security Jennie was seeing?

In contrast to the height of the entrance, the man who greeted her was her own height. Older, with a fuzzy yellow beard and a stocking cap, he looked to have been wakened from a nap.

His eyes narrowed as he asked, "What do you want?"

"I'm lost and need to find my way home."

He scoffed.

"That's what everyone who comes here wants. What is it that you need to find here?"

Jennie took a step back.

"Perhaps I have come to the wrong place. If you could tell me where there is a town nearby, I'll find my way there."

The man threw back his head laughing, almost losing the cap before he caught it in a hand that spoke of long hours at a forge, likely crafting the iron gates.

"There is no other town. You go home only if you can find your way through this one."

Jennie looked around. The mountain showed no evidence of any other humans. She'd seen no other trails from the beach.

The trail she'd been on ended here. There was nothing to do except go through.

She closed her eyes and breathed. She was tired and her mouth was dry. Surely, she'd find shelter inside. She breathed again, calming her beating heart. Something her uncle had taught her.

Her uncle. Perhaps he was the key. Or was it her mother? She thought about the last song she'd played. The out of tune note before the world shifted. What she needed was a resolution of what had gone before. She opened her eyes.

"I want to find harmony."

The man smiled.

"I am Gabriel. You have chosen well."

Reaching his hand into his pocket, Gabriel brought out three gold coins, the size of half dollars.

"You'll need these. Mind you, once they are gone, if you are not outside the gates, you will remain here indefinitely."

Jennie's blood ran cold. That sounded ominous. Three coins? Would they be enough? What would she need them for? She decided it didn't matter. She'd be back to leave once she'd rested and gotten a bit more information.

Before she could ask any questions, Gabriel disappeared back into the guard house and shut the door. She jumped as the gates squeaked and began to open outward, as if beckoning her in.

She waited until they stopped, then walked forward, slowly, looking around to see what was there.

"Get on with it."

Gabriel was now leaning out a window from the guard house inside the gate.

"There's nothing to hurt you here. The Traveler's Tavern is down the hill and on the right in town. You might want to begin your search there. The gates open for two hours if the bell rings for you. Don't forget that."

Jennie nodded, but didn't hurry forward. She'd see for herself if his words were true.

The trail expanded into a dirt road, with a sprinkle of low scrub grass and tall, brown grass on each side. A few birds cawed from a distance, which was picked up by others, who echoed the call.

Ahead she could see the beginnings of structures – a grouping of buildings that looked to be both commercial shops among a few houses. Almost as if it belonged in another time. All built of logs with thatched roofs.

Dogs ran out to greet her, jumping and barking. She shooed them away.

As she neared the first building, a woman yelled as she approached.

"Do you know where my horse is?"

A man followed her.

"I am searching for my child. Have you seen him?"

Within a minute, Jennie was surrounded by people, all asking if she'd seen someone or something. All needing something. The voices blended into a chorus that was at once its own discordant melody and a mob of voices assaulting her ears.

She threw up her hands and yelled, "STOP!"

A woman stepped back, tripping over a man's foot. Others moved back before coming toward Jennie again with the same questions.

She pushed through one side of the group, her hands up around her ears, protecting her hearing as she ran. The sounds of footsteps and indistinguishable words told her the group wasn't far behind.

On the right, just as Gabriel had said was a sign for the Traveler's Tavern.

She angled for it, dashing over the wooden sidewalk outside the doors.

Both sides swung open and Jennie ran through. The room

had two small windows at the back which let in some light, but she took a moment to let her eyes adjust. She turned to thank her saviors as they slammed the doors shut behind her.

She gasped. Standing before her was a woman who could have been her sister, with short blond hair pulled back into a bun, an apron that covered most of her flowery shirt and blue jeans and a frown on her face. The man stood to one side, at least a foot taller than Jennie and rail thin, a lazy grin on his face.

Her mother and Uncle Hugo.

"What? How?"

She shifted from looking at her mother and then back at her uncle.

Her mother shrugged, turned and went to the bar on the right side of the tavern.

Her uncle took a stop forward, his arms outstretched, folding her into his embrace.

"What are you doing here?" he asked.

Jennie fought the tears that threatened to flow.

"I don't know. One minutes I was playing the piano and the next I was on a keyboard leading to the beach."

Uncle Hugo shook his head.

"I so wish I could see it again, play on it. Hear the perfect notes flow from my fingers. Have you kept it tuned?"

Before Jennie could answer, words erupted from across the room.

"That's the way it always is. You show up here, after how many years, and all he cares about is that damn piano."

Her mother angry snarl brought back all the awful memories she'd tried to bury inside herself. As her mother turned back to cleaning the gleaming polished bar with a white cotton dishtowel, Jennie's own anger threatened to erupt. Why couldn't they get along?

"Ignore her. I'm not quite that selfish. Why are you here?"

"I honestly don't know."

His mouth became a grim line and he began to pace in front of her. The male patrons had been silently watching but now went back to drinking their mugs and playing cards without saying a word, their silhouettes fashioned from the shadows of the candles on each table and at the end of the bars.

The entire room was much like the outside, all brown walls made from logs. There weren't any women, other than Jennie's mother, which was strange. The almost quiet nature of the murmurs from the men was almost as unnerving as the crowd outside.

"That isn't how it is supposed to be. You should know why you're here. What did you tell Gabriel?" he asked.

"I told him I sought harmony."

Uncle Hugo's body seemed to become jelly-like. His arms circled wide and his back seemed to fold into itself before he righted himself. Her mother stepped away from the bar, her mouth making a large "O".

"What's the last thing you remember?"

"I was at the piano. There was a storm and lightening flashed, then the thunder roared. The high "C" note went flat, to the point that I had to cover my ears."

Jennie looked from her mother to her uncle as she saw a look pass between them.

"What? What does it mean?" Jennie asked, almost afraid they'd answer her.

"It means you're stuck here. This place isn't called Discordia for nothing. No one looking for harmony or anything like it will find it here."

Uncle Hugo let that sink in.

"Did you see those folks out here? They are here to find something too, some kind of peace or a way to come to terms with what they have lost. They may eventually get there. But you – well, you are looking to find the true note in place of the out of tune one. Maybe the solve the dissonance between your mother and me. We've been here a long time. If we can't find a way to work together for us to leave, what chance do you think you have?"

It was one of the longest speeches she'd ever heard her uncle say.

He looked defeated like she'd never seen him, even on the last day when he left their lives forever. Jennie glanced at her mother. Her shoulders were bowed and there was a sadness in her face that told her Uncle Hugo spoke the truth. Why hadn't she left the piano alone? Why had she had to play one more time?

"But that makes no sense. Where are we?"

Jennie was struggling to understand what this place was.

"I don't know exactly how this all works, but the piano and its keys, maybe with the storm's lightning, or may not, have transported you here to deal with something you cannot move on without."

Jennie stared at him. There was no such thing.

"You're lying. You and mother are dead, aren't you?

Uncle Hugo shook his head.

"For you, in this time, we are alive. I don't know why or what role we play, other than we are both tied to you. All of this is for you to solve."

Jennie moved to an open chair beside a round cherry table. A deck of playing cards with frayed edges lay next to a metal cylinder that held eating utensils. Neither interested her.

She shoved her hands in her jacket pockets. The coins. She pulled them out.

"And these? What are these for?"

"Laura?" Uncle Hugo called her mother's name for the first time Jennie had heard him use it for at least a decade. "Do you know about these?"

Jennie's mother shook her head.

"I guess you are on your own for those too."

Jennie put her head down on her arms where she rested them on the table. What the hell was she going to do?

She raised her head. She needed some sleep and some quiet time to think. Was that possible in a town where discord was the main event?

"Can I get some food and a place to sleep here?"

Uncle Hugo's head turned to check with Jennie's mother. She nodded.

"Of course, let's get you set up," he said as he moved to bring her a bowl of stew from a pot in the fireplace where it had been kept how – one Jennie was seeing for the first time. "There's beds upstairs. We don't get too many travelers here so you can have your pick."

Something about the fireplace was wrong. There was no smokey air in the tavern. The smell of the beef stew made her stomach growl and her mouth water – even as it distracted her thoughts. Jennie hadn't eaten all day.

Uncle Hugo set a glass of water beside her.

There was time enough to think about the air and explore the town later. Jennie dug into the food.

The stew was spicy with potatoes and peas, tickling her taste buds as the warm mixture soothed her body. The bowl was empty quickly.

Jennie carried the dishes to the counter where her mother stood.

"You'll do you own dishes after this meal, but for now, I'll take them."

Her mother motioned with her head towards the staircase behind the bar.

"There's a shared privy at the end of the hall. Take any of the rooms with open doors. Breakfast will be ready just past dawn. If you need anything, I sleep in the room beside the kitchen."

Her mother reached under the counter and brought out a change of clothes and nightgown.

"In case you want to use these."

Jennie's eyes teared up and she nodded. She took a few steps to the end of the counter and looked back at her mother, hoping she could give her a hug. But her mother had already started toward the kitchen.

Jennie climbed the stairs, taking the first open room, closing the door and hugging herself. The bed was a single with white sheets and a pillow in one corner and against another wall was a four-drawer dresser. A candlestick sat atop the dresser. The only other light was a square window on the same wall down from the head of the bed, the opening so small that Jennie would have barely been able to lean out of.

. She sat down on it and was surprised to find it was soft. The blanket at the end was scratchy but would be warm.

Jennie slipped out of her clothes. Her tennis shoes were still soaked with sea water and they would need to dry overnight. She pulled the nightgown over her head, feeling the tiredness in her arms. As her head hit the pillow, she slept.

The next morning, Jennie was up as the light streamed in. It was hard to imagine such a small glass paned hole could allow her to see so well, but she was grateful for it. She dressed in the clean clothes and checked her shoes.

Damp but wearable. She left them off as she headed downstairs, taking care where she stepped. She crossed to the fireplace where a new fire had already been set and was burning. Dropping her shoes in front of it, she turned back to see her mother coming out of the kitchen.

"Good, you're up. I'll bring you some oatmeal."

Jennie sat at the same table, spooning in the mixture which had been laced with cinnamon and sugar, just like she'd had as a kid. As she took a final bite, she stared into the corner of the room near the door. Following the line to the end of her uncle's bar counter.

She rubbed her eyes, not sure she was seeing correctly.

A piano? It was smaller than the one she'd left behind, but it was a piano. She turned her gaze to run down the bar, finding her uncle standing at the other end. He was shaking his head.

Jennie picked up her wooden bowl and sidestepped the other tables, making her way to the corner. She sat the bowl down and walked to the middle of the upright piano, with lovely carvings that she ran her fingers over, feeling the workmanship that had gone into the wood. Someone had polished it and kept it clean – and she knew it had to have been Uncle Hugo. Pulling the small bench barely big enough for her to sit on out, she lifted the cover on the keys.

Wood planks creaked as Jennie's uncle approached.

"Won't do no good. It's not tuned and I don't have what's needed to do that."

Uncle Hugo leaned against the wall to one side.

"Why not? Isn't there a store in town?"

"Sure is. Your mother and me, we're here for you but we can't leave this establishment."

Jennie took in his words.

"But there were people outside yesterday. I am in here now. Are you saying I can't leave?"

Uncle Hugo shook his head.

"No. You can leave but we can't. Didn't make the rules, just know that's what they are."

Jennie tested two keys. She shuddered.

Pressing more of the ivory and black keys, she found they were all out of tune. Could it be that restoring this was her way out?

"What do we need and where can I get it?"

Ten minutes later, Jennie had a list of items for restringing and repairing the instrument on a piece of paper Uncle Hugo had retrieved from one of the shelves under the counter. For a man who couldn't leave, Uncle Hugo had exact directions to the store which was four buildings down and where to find everything on her list.

A quick trip to the kitchen under the frown on her mother's face to wash the bowl and stow it on the shelf, before she retrieved her shoes which were now dry, and Jennie was off.

She opened the wooden door slowly, slipping her head out to see if anyone was on the dirt road that ran between the two lines of buildings. Seeing no one, she exited, turned right and began walking on the wood sidewalk.

Click. Click. Click.

Then more clicks.

Jennie felt the hand on her arm and swiveled around to face the woman who stepped back quickly. She was short and looked to be dressed for going to church, complete with the handbag on her arm and a lacy hat on her white curlers.

"Have you seen my dog? I lost my dog. I've been looking for so very long. Have you seen her?"

Jennie's heart went out the woman. Was she someone like Jennie, just trying to find what she needed to leave this place?

"I'm sorry. I haven't seen her, but I'll keep an eye out. What's her name?"

The woman sagged and Jennie thought she might fall. She started to reach out, but the woman straightened.

"Thank you, I can't find anyone who will help me and no one seems to know where she is. Beloved. That's her name. She's a beagle with a pink collar and silver name tag. I don't know how I'll survive without her."

Jennie nodded and turned back to her errand. She listened for footsteps so she'd know if the woman was following her but heard none. She turned back to see the woman ringing her hands as she stared into the street.

The doors to the first three buildings were shut tight, a Closed sign on each door. Jennie breathed a sigh of relief as she neared the fourth. The door was open and a man was sweeping the sidewalk with a broom.

"Can I help you? You're new to Discordia, aren't you?"

Jennie nodded and held out the paper. The man set the broom aside and turned toward the door. Jennie followed.

The store was one room, similar in size to the tavern. It was lit by the sun light coming through the dark and Jennie let her eyes adjust before moving further into the room.

A counter ran down the entire right side with shelves full of candy, fabric and notions, and a few pots and pans. Stacked bags of corn and flour were dotted against the wall across from the counter. On the back wall, there were rows of what had to be sugar and baking ingredients on the wooden shelving.

As Jennie turned back to the door, looking for the containers and stacks of tools on the left that would hold string, wire, various small metal utensils and gardening implements. As Uncle Hugo had told her, the items were exactly in the place he'd said they would be.

"Miss? I've got your items ready when you are. Feel free to look around for anything else you need."

Jennie wandered a bit, but soon was drawn to the counter where the man was adding up her purchases and tying a string around the brown paper he'd wrapped them in.

"That'll be one gold coin," he said.

For a moment, Jennie hesitated and then she pulled one out and placed it on the counter. It slid easily, gold against metal. She stared at it and resisted the urge to grab it back. Was this really what she was supposed to be spending the coins on? Could she deny Uncle Hugo a tuned piano? And what was her mother going to say?

She felt the man's eyes on her and she lifted her head. Smiling, she reached for the package, feeling the light weight, before she turned and walked out into the light.

She turned left and walked to the tavern, opening the door and walking inside. She was becoming used to moving between the dimmer inside and brighter outside.

On her right, Uncle Hugo was almost dancing with excitement. He was like a kid in a candy store who knows he's in for a treat and can barely wait.

Jennie untied the package, setting the items on the counter as Uncle Hugo opened up the piano to expose its innards. They began on the lower registers, testing each key, repairing it or tuning it as needed.

The store had not had a tuning bar nor had Uncle Hugo listed one. He'd always had perfect pitch and he used that now. Jennie had inherited that trait and between them, they found the exact adjustment needed as they moved forward.

Jennie played an ivory key, Uncle Hugo adjusted it, and they traded places. For the ones damaged, Jennie repaired one with new wire and then Uncle Hugo took the next. They developed a rhythm almost as if they were the notes in a long musical arrangement.

Across the room, Jennie could feel her mother's eyes as she set drinks before the men who played cards. Disapproval would be there and she drew back, sinking into the beat of the work.

Two hours later, the duo had completed all the work except the high "C" key.

"Would you like to do the honors?" Uncle Hugo asked. "After all, this may be the answer to what you are seeking."

Jennie stared at the key. She'd tuned the last one.

"No. I think it's right for you to do it."

He grinned.

Jennie hit the key and there was no sound.

"Could you hand that last bit of wire?"

Jennie handed it to him and stood to watch him work. With

the precision of a life-time of adjusting piano workings, he had it in place before she could sit back down. She hit the key, which was close to the sound but not quite right.

Uncle Hugo made an adjustment.

Jennie held her breath, touched the key and it fairly sang with the prefect pitch of the note.

She looked around. Nothing had changed. The air was still smokey and she was still in the tavern.

Jennie ran to the door, hoping against hope that she'd been transported back to the house. Jerking it open, the street was deserted. She hadn't gone anywhere.

Perhaps she needed to be at the gate? She dashed outside and began to run up the road. As she neared the gate, she saw that it was locked. What was it Gabriel had said? It opened for two hours when the bell ran?

There'd been no sound peals from the bell. There were none now. Only a soft wind which whispered of failure.

Jennie turned and walked back down the hill.

She opened the door to the Tavern. None of them men playing cards even turned their heads.

"It didn't work?"

Uncle Hugo was at her side.

"Nope," Jennie said as she sat down at what now seemed to be her table. "It seemed too easy but I couldn't help buy try. The good thing is that you can now play again."

He sighed.

"I can but that's not what I was hoping for either. Or your mother?"

Jennie glanced across the throom where her mother was usually behind the bar.

"What do you mean?"

"She loves you. Always has. She wanted you to find what you needed as much as I did."

Jennie found that hard to believe. Her relationship with her mother had been contentious and difficult. Jennie wanted her freedom and to do things her way. Her mother was more traditional wanting Jennie to keep to what had always been, not striving for new paths. Simpler but not as satisfying in Jennie's view. If she looked back, she could see her mother wanted what was best for her, even if Jennie didn't agree with how her mother expressed that or tried to get her to do things her way.

"I'll talk to her. I'm wondering what's for supper anyway."

Jennie pushed her chair back and walked to the bar. As if on cue, her mother appeared.

"What's for supper tonight?" Jennie asked.

"I guess Gabriel didn't tell you. The first meal is free here and after that, you can choose what you eat but you have to bring the ingredients."

Jennie frowned.

"Let me guess. The store four buildings down?"

Jennie's mother nodded.

Jennie climbed onto one of the wood barstools. She propped her elbows on the counter and set her head between her hands.

"You used to do that all the time when you were in the kitchen and trying to decide something important," her mother said as a small smile escaped before being replaced by a stony face.

"I remember. You always let me pick the dessert and sometimes the meal."

Her mother laughed, something Jennie hadn't heard in ages.

"You always wanted spaghetti. It was so easy and simple but you could never get enough of it."

Jennie's mother turned away and started for the kitchen.

"That's what I want tonight. And a cake. I'd like to help if that's okay."

Jennie waited for a response. Her mother turned and wrote

out a list of things needed on a piece of paper she had under the counter.

Jennie smiled her thanks and headed for the door.

The woman searching for her dog was on the other side of the street as Jennie hurried along to the store. While she figured the door would be open, she didn't want to chance things. She slowed as she saw the same man with the same broom still sweeping the sidewalk.

"Can I help you? You were here earlier, weren't you?"

Jennie nodded and held out the paper. The man set the broom aside and turned toward the door. Jennie followed him inside again.

As Jennie watched, he drew first one item and then another from the back wall shelved, wrapping it all up in a paper bag this time.

"That'll be one gold coin," he said.

For a moment, Jennie hesitated again, and then she pulled one out and placed it on the counter. The choice felt right although she wasn't confident this would get her home either. The best she could do was spend some time with her mother in the last place they'd been able to enjoy together.

Jennie set her purchases on the metal table in the kitchen. A wood stove sat on one wall, near the door to the outside. Counters ran on two sides with a country sink in the middle of one.

The hour of cutting onions, herbs and tomatoes for the sauce, as well heating the water for the pasta that her mother made from scratch passed quickly. Gone were the recriminations as they focused on the food and memories of time spent in the kitchen.

Jennie felt like she'd strayed into a past she'd forgotten.

With the sauce simmering on the stove, they'd whisked flour, eggs and a few other ingredients in a large wooden bowl before pouring it into an oiled and floured pan. Jennie had never baked in a fireplace, but her mother confidently moved a wire rack in place over the coals at one side for the cake.

Her mother hummed a tune as she set about making the frosting. The song was familiar and Jennie had forgotten how musical her mother had been. Those memories had been shoved aside when she began playing the piano with Uncle Hugo.

How painful that must have been since Jennie's father had played the piano as well. He'd died in a bus crash when Jennie was only four, but she remembered sitting on his lap as he played. It wasn't until Jennie was a teenager that she'd learned her father had been in a band, going on the road and leaving Jennie and her mother home to fend for themselves. Her mother had had to take whatever jobs she could after that to feed them both.

They'd moved into Uncle Hugo's house as a last effort to get back on their feet. From what her mother had said to others over the years, he held it over her. That and the death of his brother. If his brother hadn't married Jennie's mother, Uncle Hugo believed he wouldn't have died that night trying to come home to them between gigs.

Jennie wasn't sure what was true, but the cake was Uncle Hugo's favorite and she hoped he'd notice. Perhaps even make peace with her mother.

By three o'clock, Jennie was out of the kitchen. As she laid out the plain metal plates, she saw her uncle smile. She waved him over to join them as she sat down.

"I can't remember when we last had a meal together," Uncle Hugo said as he sat down.

"You wouldn't. It was the day before my husband died," Jennie's mother said as she put down the bowls of spaghetti and the sauce.

"Damn it, Laura. I lost my only brother the next day. I was

grieving when I said those things. And I've apologized over and over. What more do you want?"

Uncle Hugo had risen as he spit out the words. He slammed the chair back under the table and marched off to his side of the room.

Jennie's face had paled as she heard the words. She'd been so sure that bringing them together would get her home. Worse, she'd wasted a gold coin on the meal that she should have known was destined to fail.

She slouched into the chair.

Her mother moved behind her and put a hand on Jennie's shoulder.

"I'm sorry. That man just makes me so mad. I can't help myself. I know you wanted to fix things. Sometimes if its broken, it can't be put back together."

Jennie pushed her plate away and laid her head her crossed arms on the table. She wasn't sure whether to cry or scream at them. She'd done both over the years with no better results. A meal was a different approach that hadn't changed a thing.

She was stuck in this place with one gold coin and her family at odds. She'd walked away years ago when it was more than she could handle.

Maybe that was the answer.

Jennie filled a plate with spaghetti, covered it with sauce and walked it over to Uncle Hugo. He took it and set it on the counter.

"We weren't always at each other's throats, you know."

Jennie nodded.

"Thanks for what you were trying to do."

Jennie trudged back to the table and prepared a similar plate for her mother. As her mother came out of the kitchen, Jennie moved to the counter and set it down.

Her mother frowned and stared at the ground a moment before looking Jennie in the eyes.

"It's not that we don't care about each other, it's just too hard to be around each other. We both loved your father deeply."

Jennie leaned on the counter.

"Then why can't you find common ground in your grief?"

Her mother shrugged.

"I don't know, we just never have."

Jennie turned and walked back to the table. She had lost her appetite but needed to eat. The mixture tasted bland and she had to wash it down with water in order to swallow.

Halfway through, she put down her fork. She could continue to try to find her way home or stay here with the two people who had been the most important influences in her life. They might not be happy but they'd be together. Something those in the crowd outside looking for lost things would never have.

Jennie got up and headed to the door.

Once outside, she scanned the street. Only the woman who had lost her dog was around.

"Lady! Lady!"

The woman turned as Jennie crossed the street and ran up to her.

"Did you find my dog?"

Jennie shook her head.

"No, he's not here. You need to go home and live your life."

The woman began to cry.

"I can't. I spent my last coin trying to find her. I've no way out."

Jennie dug in her pocket.

"Take mine. I've decided to stay."

From across the street, Jennie's mother and Uncle Hugo had opened the tavern door.

"No. Keep it. You'll need that to go home."

Jennie ignored her family's pleas.

"I know how important something you love is. Please take it

and go home."

The woman grabbed the coin and hugged Jennie.

"You don't know how much this means to me. Thank you."

Jennie smiled, relief pouring through her that she no longer had to decide on what to do. The money was gone and so was her ability to leave.

She walked back across the street.

"What the hell were you doing?" Uncle Hugo asked. "That was your ticket out of here."

"For once, Hugo and I are in agreement. You shouldn't have done that."

Jennie looked at them both, smiled, and moved to sit at the round table.

"I think it's time for the cake."

Jennie's mother stared at Jennie. She headed to the kitchen and returned with the cake. Cutting three pieces, she put one on each plate.

A bell rang, its peal sending shivers down Jennie's back.

"That's good news."

"What's that?" Uncle Hugo asked.

"The bell. I can hear it ringing. I guess that lady is on her way home now."

Jennie watched Uncle Hugo and her mother look at each other.

"The only one who can hear the bell is the one it rings for. That bell is yours. You need to hurry. Change back into your clothes and get to the gate."

Jennie breathed in deeply. She wasn't sure what was happening, only that she had a chance to leave. She stood up and headed to the stairs. Changing quickly, she was back down in a few minutes where she stood in the middle of the tavern trying to decide what to do.

Her mother was the first to approach.

"I always regretted that we didn't stay close. My gift to you is our memories – of the good times. Leave the others behind and move on with the happy ones."

Jennie fell into her mother's arms, wishing she could stay there but knowing she had to leave.

Uncle Hugo stepped up to take her into her arms.

"The relationship between your mother and me was always our issue, not yours. Go, knowing that I love you and remember me each time you sit at a piano."

Waves of grief seemed to roll over Jennie. She was losing them all over again.

Together, her mother and uncle said, "Go. We have lived our lives. It is time for yours. Be happy and move forward instead of staying in the past."

Jennie took a final look and ran outside. She hiked up the hill, seeing the gate open.

"So, you found what you were looking for?" Gabriel asked.

"I think so."

"Good. Hold onto it so you don't have to come back. And hurry forward, there's a storm at sea."

Jenny hurried down the path, the rocks and sand sliding beneath her feet. She fell on her bottom once, but picked herself up. She continued.

The further down the hill she went, the darker the day had become. Black thunderclouds had rolled in.

At the large rock at the end of the path, she climbed up and for the first time, took stock of what she faced.

The storm was raging. Rain had begun and Jennie would have to cross the smaller rocks, slick from the rain. The sulphury seawater smell was back. Lightning flashed across the sky, blinding her at times. The thunder roared in her ears.

Jennie ignored it all, focusing on moving from rock to rock.

She jumped from the last rock onto the packed sand area, avoiding the sand that was shifting and that she sunk one foot into when she first arrived on the beach.

Her clothes began to cling to her from the rain and the sea spray.

The keyboard was almost covered in water. All she could see where the last few keys of the highest register on a piano. The high "C" was almost hidden, with water washing back and forth over it.

Jennie suddenly understood. She took a step back and ran, feeling the water seep into her tennis shoes again before she jumped.

She brought all of her weight down on the high "C" key.

The pure pitch perfect note resounded through the air, resonating within Jennie as she once again closed her eyes and clasped her hands over her ears. A flash of light that penetrated her eyelids lit up the sky and the thunder boomed.

Then all was silent.

Jennie removed her hands and opened her eyes. She was back at the piano in her old home.

Jennie stared out the window where the storm was breaking up. She could already see a bit of blue sky as the clouds were being driven off by a light wind.

She placed her fingers on a key and hit a note. It rang back true. She tried another with the same result.

A wave of relief rolled over her as she realized that it was time to let go of the piano and the house. She'd take with her the memories of the good and the bad, but mostly of the good. Neither her mother or her uncle's decisions in life could rule her choices and from now on, she wouldn't feel guilty about not keeping what they had insisted had to stay as it always had.

She laughed at herself. She wasn't sure how she'd fallen asleep. What an amazing dream that had been. And so cathartic. She felt lighter than she had in years.

Jennie stood up and looked down. Her tennis shoes were wet.

ABOUT THE AUTHOR

C.A. Rowland loves traveling and learning about cultures, whether they are exotic ones or small-town life. Ms. Rowland has explored countless places from empty neighborhood houses to Roman ruins that seem to draw her. Those travels inspired many of her stories. Raised in Texas, she now calls Tennessee home – a place of history and folklore.

Ms. Rowland writes historical fiction, science fiction, fantasy, and mysteries. Her first amateur sleuth paranormal mystery novel, *The Meter's Always Running* was published in 2020. She comes by her interest in ghosts, myths, and legends and the paranormal naturally, having spent hours in cemeteries with her grandmother.

Her work can also be seen in several volumes of *Fiction River* and *Pulphouse Magazine,* as well as other anthologies.

You can keep up with her upcoming fiction and travel adventures at www.carowland.com.

Hope to see you there!

ALSO BY C.A. ROWLAND

<u>Novels:</u>

The Meter's Always Running

<u>Short Stories:</u>

8 Seconds

A Rite of Passage

Prairie Dog Town Maude and the Hurricane (a Texas tall tale)

The History of a Fruitcake

The Remembrance

Visit www.carowland.com for information on my newest releases, my stories in other anthologies, and my travels and the inspiration for my stories. Hope to see you there!

STEPPING THROUGH...

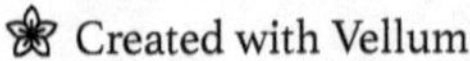 Created with Vellum